Always Here

S.L. Mauldin

ALWAYS HERE by S.L. Mauldin
Published by TouchPoint Press
www.touchpointpress.com

ISBN-10: 1-946920-23-1
ISBN-13: 978-1-946920-23-2

Editor: Kimberly Coghlan
Book Cover Design: Todd Redner
Front Cover Photo: Hagen Mattingly
Back Cover Photos: Terri Warren and Susan Petteway

First Edition

Printed in the United States of America.

It was a dream team and I thank you Kelly Sirois, Hagen Mattingly, Eric Hernandez, Stella Doyle, Jonathan Matthews, Cate Petteway, Gabbi Fairey, Tony Veller, Ty Redner, Javy Barahona, Austin Griffis Jillian Melko, Jason Gaglione, Jackson Wright, Savannah Carmichael, and Sydney Warren. Much appreciation to the mothers, fathers and grandmothers of those listed above! Ditto for Caroline Whiskersley, Kita Blodwen, Devan Gilbert, Terri Warren and James Sirois. Thank you Todd Redner for the stunning cover. Thank you Blank Stage Acting Studios - Anthony, Brent, Lillian, Baby James and all your thespians who served as extras. Thank you Susan Petteway for all the behind the scenes assistance!

EPILOGUE

An X stood out in my view, with a long, thick black line next to it. Printed in bold lettering was my full birth name: Miranda Leigh Owens. The hands of my family members rested along a lengthy, wooden conference table. Some hands quietly clasped together while others tapped anxiously. My hand visibly trembled as I willingly lowered the pen towards the daunting document, and as the ink nearly touched the blaring white, I hesitated.

To my right, a tender hand with aged skin eased across the table in my direction and rested pleasantly on my free arm. My grandmother, Nana made the supportive gesture in efforts to calm my rattled nerves. I love that about her. Despite the comforting motion, my thoughts wandered back to the point that landed me here in the first place. The room grew cold, and then I faintly detected the sound of "Always here" emanating from a comforting, familiar voice.

One

Christian always ran several minutes late, though I'll never understand why because it wasn't like he wheeled around town in a sluggish four-cylinder Honda Civic; he drove a fast car. It ticked Christian off, and as much as I tried, my memory failed to remember the make of that car. Cars were his thing—not mine. At times, I wondered if he ever realized that I am a female. Was the semblance of boobs not enough? I mean, I wasn't getting calls from an orphanage to come over for a feeding, but still… While I was waiting, I thought about such things.

My detail about the car remained limited to recalling that it was humungous, built in the early seventies, and according to him, a properly restored vehicle that held a four-hundred and some odd number engine. The specifics in regards to the motor size, I knew intimately since Christian constantly revved up the engine while proudly announcing, "Four-hundred blah blah block baby." Beats me what was so fascinating about that number, but if that made his engine tick, then so be it. In addition, he bragged about the fact of its status of being a muscle car, but I pondered what muscles had to do with anything. It was just a car. Although, I could attest to the fact that the doors were extremely heavy and hard to swing open, but as far as I was concerned, I saw no muscles from them. Perhaps gaining muscle mass is a building effect after repetitiously opening and closing the doors over a longer period of time, and Christian had only had the car for a year. Time would tell.

Christian was just as meticulous with his hair as he was with his car. Very few times had I ever witnessed the muscle car without a freshly swiped coat of tire shine, and his brown locks were always groomed as though a personal attendant might maintain each strand.

Since being accustomed to Christian's behavior, it was not so odd to me when my best friend whipped out a spray bottle of window cleaner, spritzed the interior of the front windshield, and wiped the window with a cloth while we waited for a traffic signal to blink to green. Other drivers composed text messages while Christian sprayed and wiped like a compulsive madman. Typically, he concluded his ritual by surveying his quiff in the rearview mirror where he intensely checked each side of his head and the free willed strands that landed just center of his forehead. Of course, following that, Christian wiped the edges of the mirror because fingerprints from the gel or something might drive him crazy, I suppose. Both actions seemed downright OCD in my evaluation.

A girly-girl who obsessed with such things as mirrors, brushes, or makeup wasn't an adequate way to describe aspects of my personality.

I possessed many of my own quirks though: one of which involved repetitively glancing out of my bedroom window checking to see if Christian's car was waiting in the drive. Only when I expected him though. Still, checking was truly silly because I could hear the muscle car's engine growling from two streets over, which allowed me plenty of time to gather my stuff and meet him out in front of my house.

Anticipation lived with me constantly—anticipation that something good was hiding just around the corner or a tragedy was bound to catch up with me when I least expected the event. One wall in my room held a huge window, which made it easy enough to observe the entire cul-de-sac, just in case the impending event happened to be skipping across the treetops in suburbia.

We moved into the neighborhood when I was six, and from what little I can recount, I remember begging mom and dad to let me take this particular room where I had now slept for ten years. The world presented itself as a much larger place when I was four-foot tall, standing on the tips of my toes, and looking upward. At the time, the oversized view made me feel like I was living in a grand castle—the kinds dominating stories about princes and princesses. Shrinking over the decade as the trees in the neighborhood grew taller, my mansion became eerily similar to a majority of homes in other middleclass communities of America where there are no large stone blocks, lookout towers, drawbridges, or water filled moats.

Still waiting. On the fifth quick glance out of the window, there was no shiny car painted fire engine red. Outside, activities were limited to our neighbors on several sides whacking, blowing, and mowing for what appeared as a frantic battle to have the best-looking lawn on the street of look-a-like homes.

Despite our neighbors' desperate ambitions, there was always that one house desperately in need of minor repair, painting, and a landscape overhaul, and dad often shared his opinions saying he believed those sorts of dwellers should stick to apartment rentals. He remained adamant that if they insisted on living in a neighborhood, they should at least consider one with a HOA that provided a lawn care service included with the price of their monthly dues. According to him, home values dropped when one house on the block sat in disarray. Whatever that is about.

Hearing dad discuss these facts with my mom every time we passed 104 Hampton in the car, the topic was so played out. "One zero four Hampton: gosh, the house with the flaking paint and curled shutters;

what are we to do?" On the exterior of the troublesome house, one of the two front porch lights tilted to the right, which wore on dad's last nerve like nothing else. Once, I think he even slipped a scathing note inside the homeowner's mailbox with a list of suggestions that would improve their curb appeal and the street's net worth. However, after those suggestions, I decided the defiant homeowners left everything as is for spite. Thank God dad had no knowledge of their email address because the results would've made for an interesting inbox once he launched an inclusive campaign with the competing neighbors. Clearly, a Lifetime movie in the making where a neighborhood intends to reinvent their town when one suggestive email leads to a man's murder with a garden shovel. Well, that's if owners of the curling shutters even had gardening equipment at all; it was hard to tell.

Still waiting. Still thinking. On my sixth glance, two newly trained bicycle riders circled the turnaround as the small machinery buzzed so loudly that I could clearly hear them even with headphones tightly tucked in my ears. After a seventh look from my second floor penthouse, I figured Christian was detained at a nearby carwash putting another glossy layer on the car tires following a thorough wash and hand dry. Heaven forbid if we showed up at the mall in a dirty classic.

Taking off my headphones, I docked my iPod while raising the volume level as high as it would go. Before pressing play, I grabbed a flatiron off a dressing table since it served as the perfect microphone.

Surrounded by my four-walled fortress, I could be anything or anyone I wished to be. The many stuffed animals I'd outgrown, and hardly ever paid any attention to, served as my audience, just as they had since first grade. With my friendly crowd of onlookers, I performed with abandonment on a short worn path of carpet in front my dressing table that functioned as my stage...and for a few minutes, I escaped. During my short performance, my long, lost button-eyed companions would have my attention once again.

While in my mother's car one afternoon, I fell in love with The Go Go's, an all-girl band from the eighties. I surmise they were popular in her day, and listening to their tunes reminded Mom of a time in her youth before stress became a dominate force in her life. My mother was extremely conservative, but I have suspicions that she might've partied a little in her time. Nowadays, she kept her excitement contained to moving her lips and a vaguely visible finger tap on the steering wheel. I don't even think she was ever aware of her movements until she caught me watching her out of the corner of my eye, which caused her to slip back into statue mode. Twenty years earlier, I bet she'd let her head flip from side to side and actually let lyrics come out of her mouth with sound. I mean is this what happens? We grow up, we have children, and we become stuffed animals simply going through the motions of life. One bland expression, one stare, and a life sitting in the same chair staring forward waiting for something to happen?

Since hearing the oldies, I'd downloaded quite a few of The Go Go's songs and added them to my play list favorites. Strangely, five days after the fact, I caught wind that Mr. Stancil, my schools drama teacher, had written a musical called, "The Whole World Lost its Head." Inspiring the piece, Mr. Stancil had read Belinda Carlisle's "Lips Unsealed" during a short trip to New York City to catch some shows on Broadway. Belinda is the former lead singer of The Go Go's. His idea left me intrigued, and I wanted to be involved. One problem though: I'm shy. Me in front of a group that isn't stuffed with cotton, adorned with buttons, and googling eyes, no way. Nevertheless, the coincidence left me wondering about the universe and its constant nudging to go in a certain direction. Is my voice meant for more than the shower and the motionless listeners sitting attentively together in a white wicker chair?

Ever since I heard about Mr. Stancil blending the magic of "Mama Mia" and a candid tale from a girl rock star, I obsessively discussed the matter with Christian. If Christian had boobs or more importantly, a singing voice, he would have jumped at the chance to try out for the musical. The only harmonizing he could muster involved the purr of something fueled by gasoline and motor oil.

Gripping the pretend microphone, I instructed Mr. Bear and friends to hold the applause until the end of the show. I pressed play; the riff began, and lyrics followed. "The freeway fell into the bay..."

Moving back and forth in front of the large window, I belted into the flatiron, moving my head from side to side. Out of the corner of my eye, I noticed that the two young cyclists paused just short of the lawn. They'd removed their protective helmets, and along with my stuffed friends, they watched my spontaneous performance. From what I could tell, they all posed the same blank expression, but I wondered if this were a good shock or a bad shock? For a shy girl who wished to do some kind form of performing as a career, my audience's bland faces weren't very encouraging.

I floated around the sleeping quarters trying my best to mimic a dance I'd seen in old eighties music videos. For me, the dance resembled someone trying to chop iceberg lettuce while gripping large chef knives in both hands. The leg movements I had trouble getting it down; it's as if they were buckling from underneath a person; one knee went inward as the other went outward. Try coordinating that with a head of lettuce and two arms swinging sixteen-inch silver blades. Belinda's voice and mine melded. "Has the whole world lost its head-is it just me?"

Getting lost in the song, I spun around; when suddenly, out of nowhere, heavy streams of canned whipping cream pelted me in the face.

Stunned, I stuttered, "I I I."

Dropping the microphone as I feverishly wiped both sides of my face, my brother's bff Nathan reached into his back pants pocket ripping out his cell phone. He lifted it upwards and held it out in front of him pressing the application to capture my desperate image.

"I got to post this on Facebook and Instagram."

I lunged forward with every effort in an attempt to slaughter them both, Nathan and my younger brother Greer. Blinded by the whipped topping, I managed to get a grasp on someone's shirt, but they were able to pull away from my slippery grip. By the time, I cleared the topping from my eyes, the two of them had scampered out of my room, and shortly after, I heard an exterior door shutting downstairs. Slamming my bedroom door, I shifted direction, leaned my back against it, and slid down to the carpet. Using my finger, I took a taste of the whip cream, and the sweetness made me smile, but it was only for a second before I screamed loudly.

****

After exiting the house, Nathan and Greer kick flipped their skateboards from the ground up into their arms.

Nathan maneuvered his hat backwards. "What a loser!"

Reaching the end of the driveway, Nathan and Greer tossed the skateboards onto the ground and jumped on causing the wheels to roll forward as the gravel crunched underneath the weight. The two young bike riders were still watching the action play out from the edge of the cul-de-sac as Greer wheeled the board in their direction, skidded sideways, and came to a stop.

"Hey, what are you two turds up to? What gives? Spill it you two June bugs before Nathan and me make a close introduction of your faces to the lawn."

The young bikers had nothing to tell other than that they were watching Miranda dance. When the harassing was over, Nathan and Greer showed off their boarding skills as they skated away from the boys. It didn't take long for the two small cyclists to put on their helmets and resume their shaky jaunt around the encircled black pavement.

Struggling with their skateboards and almost at the top of a hill, a familiar engine's roar grew clearer, and when the two best friends reached the peak, a sports car appeared in the prankster's view.

Paused at a four-way stop, music thrummed from inside Christian's vehicle. Through the front window, Christian noticed Nathan and Greer jumping onto their skateboards just ahead of him. Christian revved the engine, and the car heaved up and down while Nathan and Greer started descending the hill, picking up speed.

Nathan removed his hat and shoved the bill in a back pocket. "There's your buddy."

Greer followed suit, removing his hat. "Good, we got away from my house just in time."

Nathan's board swayed from side to side. "Does your sister think he is her boyfriend or something?"

"No, she doesn't. Her brain isn't completely sunken. It still floats. She thinks he is her sister."

Laughing, Nathan gestured. "Good one! Since I was nine, I thought you were her sister."

Grabbing a chunk of his butt, Greer responded. "Choke on a cheek chump!"

Glancing in the rearview mirror, Christian smoothed strands of hair with each hand on both sides of his head. Then with two fingers, he ran the length of hair collected between and just above his eyebrows. When he finished, Christian adjusted the mirror and used a handy-wipe to clean the edges. All the while, Christian continued eyeing the two skaters zooming down the incline heading in his direction.

"Now is my chance to do mankind a huge favor. Maybe not death. Just an arm, a leg. I wonder what the punishment would be. Too bad, I couldn't get their lips on the ground. Splat. Only mumbles, no more words. What about other body parts? What about reproductive organs? No offspring. I'd be a hero."

Revving the engine once more, Christian eased a foot from the brake pedal. The cherry red muscle car began spinning forward at a rapid rate. Left behind at the four-way were clouds of dust and burned rubber markings on the hard pavement. The four hundred and some odd engine number powered the car up the hill with ease using its 340 horsepower.

Aware of the car briskly heading in their direction, Nathan and Greer scrambled to get out of the way. As the car sped past the two of them where they were sheltered on the side of the street, Christian's hand bolted out the side window waving until the car reached one-hundred feet away.

Reaching down, Greer lifted the skateboard off the grass. "What was that about?"

Nathan retrieved his hat and placed it on his head. "He was in a hurry because someone sent him a text message telling him about a sale on hair products at the mall."

Christian eased up on the accelerator. "Should've taken them out. I've got to buck up."

Looking in the rearview mirror, Christian caught sight of Nathan and Greer making obscene hand gestures from behind. Without thought, he stomped on the break, shoved the gear shifter in reverse, and throttled the heavy car backwards, leaving scorched pavement and smoke. Once again, Nathan and Greer scrambled to take cover from the storm heading in their direction.

Two

My family held a few pranksters in the mix. Between Nana, my fourteen-year-old brother, and me, someone was always trying to one-up the other with clever trickery. Mostly, it was Nana and I teaming up on Greer for revenge. However, he was so sneaky with his deception, he always caught us when we least expected an attack. In that respect, Greer was winning the full on skirmish on the battlefield.

Even though Christian was on his way to pick me up, I had no options but to take a quick shower. Unless I wanted to have bees following me around all day or even worse smelling of soured dairy, it was necessary to wash off the remnants of the sugary assault from earlier.

For once, Christian's tardiness worked in my favor for three reasons. As I said, a quick shower and two, the distraction saved me from gazing out of the window constantly. Lastly, I conjured a surprise for Greer. I'm sure my button-eyed friends wouldn't mind an early exit to stage left, and from their expression, it seemed they hardly noticed.

For days, I'd pondered the safety of the ideal prank, but due to my frustration caused by the rude interruption of my performance, I decided to go for it. I mean, what was the worst thing that could happen really? 911 was just a call away, and they had a pretty good track record for promptness I think.

Removing the plastic caps from both of the tubes carefully, I placed the openings of the two containers together. Slowly, using my right hand, I squeezed, and the wasabi paste oozed across the bridge and into the toothpaste side. I capped both containers and then I positioned the toothpaste tube on the counter. Then, using my finger, I applied pressure to various points to mix the wasabi and toothpaste together inside the tube.

"Exhilarating. Eye Opening and refreshing."

Completing my task just in time, I heard the rumble of the muscle car—whatever it is called. A tire squealed, so obviously Christian had recklessly pulled in the drive and parked. Grabbing my things, I headed for the door.

The scent of rubber melting hit me the second I closed the front door of the castle. It was no surprise that I saw Christian checking his look in the mirror. I'd told him several times it wasn't wise to drive with both windows down if he was so concerned about his hair being blown out of place. There was no air conditioning in the oldie, so not only did it help with toning the arms, during warmer weather, the classic served as a sauna as well. Believe me when I say that car was toasty—but in a different sense than when Christian calls it hot.

Christian positioned the rear view mirror. "Chickie."

I squeezed my backpack on the floor to the left of my feet and shut the door. "That smell is?"

"Roadkill."

"Anyone I know?"

Christian faced me with a look. "Miranda, you know I don't discriminate."

"True."

"Seatbelt!"

It drove me mad when Christian spoke those quick words of warning, especially in front of my parent's house since I knew what was to follow, and I was thankful that they were away at that moment. Saturdays involved mom and dad's ritualistic visit to a home improvement store and the local grocer for the weekly gathering of forage.

At the do it yourself store, while they carted each aisle, I'm sure that my dad pointed out to my mother how cheaply 104 Hampton could clean up their neighborhood eyesore. In that regards, the only idea that modified every few years was what color he would choose to paint the body of the deteriorating house, but staying consistent, Dad's choice of trim color remained Divine White. No doubt, styles had changed several times since our community's trees were saplings ten years ago.

Urgently, I grappled for the seatbelt. In unison with my movement, Christian flung the gear shifter to the R position causing the transmission to buzz as the engine growled with life. By now, I should've known to be prepared for the sudden jolt from our launch pad. I pleaded that the mini motors involved in the lawn competition might distract the competitors from noticing the gray smoke lingering around our mailbox, let alone the noise generated as the tires violently reacted with the asphalt. With any luck, the smell of freshly cut grass might disguise the scent of scorched pavement and melting rubber.

When we neared the top of a hill in the neighborhood and crawled to a stop at the four-way, I noticed my brother and Nathan at the bottom of the hill. Still riding skateboards at fourteen? I mean, really?

I motioned my finger. "Now, there is some worthy road kill."

"Took that elevator already." Christian's hands flexed around the steering wheel.

"I still see mobility. What happened?"

"Oh, you know me. Taking the high road."

Christian hit the gas as an intense focus took over his face.

The car's momentum passed Nathan and Greer as Christian and

Miranda waved out of each of the side windows.

Greer phased back out onto the street. "That cotton swab shouldn't be allowed to drive."

Nathan added. "Preach."

"So, where did you say this place is again?"

Greer tossed the skateboard to the ground. "In the brick building next door to the pharmacy."

"What pharmacy?"

"The one where you got that cream to clear up that nasty rash you had on your groin."

Nathan peered around. "Dude! Don't say stuff like that so loud. People around here gossip. What if that got back to my mother?"

"She'd ask you about your rash?"

"Dude, I never had a rash."

"Don't tell me; tell your mother when she asks."

****

We made a safe landing at the mall, and after many laps around the lot, we discovered a parking spot that suited all of Christian's requirements. Rule number one: no parking next to mini-vans because that indicated the presence of children. Children are clumsy enough and moms are even clumsier while unfolding their multi-talented strollers. Rule number two: parking next to trucks more than ten-years-old indicated the presence of a hillbilly and their temptation to press their hands against the window of his car and look inside was too great. Rule number three: no parking next to cars that presented any combination of Grand, Avenue, Park, or Marquis because that driver had many past birthdays and their vision was most likely waning in their twilight. Optional Rule number four: Sometimes a vehicle's sticker value applied as well. Like I mentioned, completely OCD!

I didn't oppose when Christian insisted on Mediterranean for lunch. It was the typically the shortest line since all the other middleclass mall dwellers ritualistically gathered in front of chains who specialized in clogged arteries and lubricated meat. The fact that they needed to add an additive so that diners could easily swallow their food made my decision simple.

As we meandered through the sea of automobiles, Christian playfully informed me of all the cars that were in complete violation of all the rules. Once inside the mall, Christian halted the banter long enough to order miso chicken with brown rice, and that lasted a mere four minutes. At that point, my best friend shifted to speculation as to which person waiting for meatless meat in a bun drove which offensive vehicle.

Once we seated ourselves and my best friend caught his breath, the subject of exasperating parking considerations shifted. In relations to my enthusiasm about the school musical, Christian was convicted that I could handle taking it on. For an entire week, Christian had been urging me to audition for Mr. Stancil. With food in hand, he stated his case one more time.

Christian lifted his first bite. "What kind of name is Pam anyway? Is she named after a cooking spray?"

"Well, she is slippery."

"I still say you should do it. It's a step towards what you want to do with your life right?"

I rolled my eyes. "Why not a little more humiliation in the front of all the other high school idiots? Right?"

"You have just as good of a chance."

"Different price tags."

"Chickie, she is only a day sale away from being on the clearance rack."

"Twenty years from today, we can rejoice when her waistline

resembles an oversized belt made out of ice cream and sadness."

Pausing, Christian pondered. "What, you don't think she will still be rationing one stalk of celery per day?"

"Are you kidding? You know how those girls are. The fantasy. Ken to their Barbie. Diapers. PTA. There are track records for how they all end up."

Pushing away his food, Christian added. "Bloated, admiring the Jenny Craig spokesperson and shopping for every unproven age cream on the market."

"Sales in the billions even. Not for me."

"Miranda, think about it? You have to trust me. You've got what it takes. Remember our pact"

"The pact?"

"Miranda, you don't remember the pact we made in third grade?"

"I hardly remember what I did yesterday."

Christian leaned in. "We said we would be there for each other no matter what."

"Oh yeah. How'd that go again?"

"Through math, through art—even through death, we won't part."

Christian rested his fork long enough to show me his half of the friendship pendant on his necklace. "You should do it because you know I will be right there with you in spirit."

Smiling, I responded sarcastically. "What shall I wear?"

"Good. You can start looking for something theatrical while I look for shoes."

"Since you're OCD and ADD, that should give me plenty of time for sure. And what does something theatrical look like?"

Pam was that girl, the popular one. Why everyone fawned over her was a question left unanswered. Sure, she was cute, and so were other girls at school, but that special spark that set her apart from the others, well I couldn't see it. Lest they forget that in second grade, Pam was a chunky little seven-year-old. I remembered it. That was about the last time that I spoke with her. I remembered it vividly. She showed up at school one day with the most adorable backpack fashioned around some popular character at the time. That must have been the element that gave her an advantage in the popularity game—and suddenly a reason to ignore my existence. We had a new mortgage to pay, so I had to survive with standardized single color zip and tote.

According to the yearbooks, Pam socialized with every worthy club at school, served on the student council, and had the lead role in any form of theatrical performance. Christian noted many conspiracy theories about those facts and questioned why the Drama Department even bothered to hold auditions at all. I would have to say that it had crossed my mind, but her parents buying off the staff was only a theory so, I would need proof in order to believe it, yet it was totally plausible.

****

Half an hour later, Nathan and Greer arrived at the music school situated in the middle of a strip-mall. Nathan's one obsession since he had entered high school was Pam. Though she was slightly older, the full force of puberty and reeling hormones blinded Nathan's vision to seeing anything other than his end goal. In that, he was convinced Pam would fall madly in love with him if she ever heard his voice. Countless hours that should've been dedicated to homework were consumed by investigating Pam's whereabouts and following her every move. Not yet a victim of a crippling disease called girl crazy, Greer served as Nathan's wingman in the quest to get the girl.

Nathan removed his hat. "Dude, how did you find out she goes here?"

"I've got my sources."

Inside, Pam practiced her vocals with the coach she had trained with since she was little girl. “Tra la la la la.”

“Again.”

Looking at his image in the reflective window outside the music school, Nathan used a little spit and his fingers in attempts to make his hat-head vanish as Greer stretched for the front door. Nathan twirled his skateboard around and rested it against the exterior wall. “Just be cool.”

“Oh young hopeful fool.” Greer laughed.

“Don’t be a hater.”

Greer nudged Nathan’s shoulder, “Skater not a hater.”

A glass partition separated a waiting section from the rehearsal area of the school. Nathan and Greer chose a spot in the long row of seating in the visitors’ area.

“Just look at her.” Nathan fixated on Pam.

“Isn’t that why we’re here?”

Behind the glass, Pam reached for her purse that rested on a nearby stool as the voice coach handed Pam a sheet of paper.

“You can work on those steps at home.”

Pam made her way to exit the studio. Nathan’s mind floated away to wonderland, and the approaching object of his infatuation provoked detectable anxiety. The door swung outward toward the lobby as Nathan swallowed trying to clear the four-wheeled ATV that was making its way down his throat. Or so it felt. Greer remained level headed, but he wasn’t the one bitten by the love bug.

Flirting seemed a natural attribute, though she was completely unaware, as Pam mimicked the behavior of her mother. Unknowingly, her skills had been under development since a very early age.

“Hey guys.” Walking by, Pam’s head swirled and her long hair with varying shades of blond collected over one shoulder.

There was no reason for the boys to be surprised since Pam

typically said hi to everyone with whom she came in contact.

Nathan's arm spastically flung outward to the side catching Greer in the chest. Caught off guard, Greer winced; his ribs made a thud sound, and his mouth hurled an uhhggh.

Greer managed to speak up. "Hi."

With a friendly smile, Pam heaved the exit door. "See you later."

Nathan and Greer quickly retrieved their skateboards and followed Pam, as newly born puppies would do.

Outside, a car reversed out of a parking spot, and Nathan and Greer stalled watching as the car exited the retail shopping center. Nathan tugged his pocketed hat and mounted it on his head.

"Dude, she totally said hi to me."

Curiously, Greer peered at his best friend. "She said hi to you?"

"Didn't you hear her?"

Greer's hand swooped, and two fingers smoothed one eyebrow. "Reel yourself in fly fisher."

Dazed, Nathan commented. "Oh man, she said hi to me."

Greer smoothed a second brow. "Why didn't you say hi back?"

Puzzled by the question, Nathan glared at Greer. "Dude, don't you know anything about girls? Don't want to come on too strong."

Greer pitched his skateboard onto the ground and hopped on. "Clever, tadpole! If you don't talk to her, there is no way it's going to happen."

****

We managed to spend six hours at the mall shopping. I stopped counting how many pairs of shoes Christian tried on after number seven. It was ridiculous. Even after numerous different styles, he left empty handed. Myself, well, I bought a few things, but only out of necessity. Jeans can only last so long, and I actually had had a growth spurt right after the new school year started, so the ones I purchased at the end of the summer were creeping up to floodwater status. I survived the backpack alienation, but I don't think I would overcome the torture of being constantly questioned as if I were waiting for a flood or if I had plans to go fishing.

In between loafers and running shoes, Christian continued his rant about the audition. I continued tossing puns until the universe threw out a take notice. Since when did they start doing karaoke at the mall? Some emo-girl was ruining a classic. I couldn't help but take it as a sign when "We Got the Beat" echoed through the open spaces of the enclosed shopping arena. I made a decision. The Go Go's were calling. If I had had a large group of friends, it would've been the ideal moment for a spontaneous flash mob.

How could I do this and retain my dignity? Going head to head with a non-stick aerosol named Pam? My shield wasn't made out of Teflon, and obviously, Pam didn't need to protect her surface from anything sticky.

****

Perching in the middle of the bed with my laptop, I stared blankly at the empty application. If only the screen suddenly had had a pop-up with clear indications—a message from the universe. I waited, but nothing happened, so it had to be the pop-up blockers stopping the alert. Oh, perfect timing for them to actually work.

Name? What is my name? I couldn't remember. I laughed. That's a great excuse; I'd tell Christian I had onset amnesia. Surely, he'd believe me when I said it's a genetic condition with no known medical solution. I pecked at the keys slowly while watching the letters connect together to spell out my full name.

Another sign came—or at least I took it that way. Within seconds of hearing water flowing through the plumbing in the walls, I heard Greer singing in the shower. Not good singing though; he sounded like he had a large bar of soap crammed in his mouth. Nevertheless, he was singing. Was his voice cracking? Teenaged boys going through puberty sounds hilarious. One minute they are a little boy, the next minute, it sounds as though someone is squeezing a duck by the neck.

The well-earned payback about to go down excited me and urged my fingers to move quickly along keyboard. Why are you auditioning? What kind of question is that? Is that not a given? Is this a trick question? After hitting submit, I neared the bedroom door, sat down on the floor, and placed my ear snuggly against the wall.

I attempted visualizing whatever was happening behind that closed bathroom door. The water ceased whining through the pipes. By now, Greer was drying off his skinny and pale pubescent body. His hair most likely spiked upward, I assumed because often he left the bathroom strutting like a mentally challenged peacock.

Starting with five, I counted backwards in my head until I reached the number one. The impressive wail began and sounded like a ten-year-old boy, almost a girl. As the seconds passed, the screams cracked and transformed into a more masculine plea for help.

I lifted off the floor when I heard feet pounding up the wooden steps of the stairwell just outside my door. As I eased open the bedroom door, both my parents were rushing down the hall toward the bathroom, where it sounded as though someone were nearing death. I followed them, and for a moment, I worried that I'd taken things too far. I'm not exactly sure how long it took emergency services to travel to our neighborhood. Hopefully, not too long. Though Greer was a complete pest, I'd rather him not die. If he experienced a little pain, well, I had no problem with that situation. Actually, a lot of pain might've been okay too. However, he wasn't worth going to jail over.

My dad slid the bathroom door open; the whimper got louder when I peeked around my mother's shoulder. Then I wasn't so worried. If I'd ever needed restraint, this was the moment. Laughter brewed deep down inside, and I couldn't stop it. Bending over the vanity, clad in skimpy tighty-whities, Greer spastically shoveled water from the faucet towards his mouth. His wet spiked hair bumped the mirror leaving behind an interesting pattern that resembled splattered-paint artwork. He looked like a complete tool. However, he was breathing, gasping even, which was a good thing. No jail time for me.

I tried, but holding it in, forget it. It was like vomit rising up and out and spreading all over. Along with spittle, a roaring giggle blurted from my clenched mouth. Completely confused, my parents turned and stared at me with a questionable brow. Greer's head tilted to one side as he continued feverishly cupping water into his hole to quell the fire. By his expression, I knew it to be a declaration of war. Could I handle it on two fronts—a war at school with a bakery lubricant and a war with the homeland prankster?

****

Pam knew three different versions of her boyfriend. The one she fell for, a kind stocky football player, who said things to her that she needed to hear. His counter self was a boy who behaved appropriately with parents or around persons of authority. Becoming more constant, seeping through the cracks, lived an angry individual who couldn't control his tongue or his temper, and Pam had visited with them all.

The first boy lured Pam in with praise, something she lacked in her home life. He easily filled the need that her pretentious parents didn't meet. Manipulating his way out of any situation, the second personality charmed in a different way: if only to distract anyone from peering deeper inside. Inside, hiding from detecting eyes, a monster lay dormant and peeked out on occasion. But that creature became more easily aroused; he kept one eye open, one paw cocked, and he remained ready to pounce.

Pam's mother gracefully scooted a wingback chair underneath the antique table centered in the posh dining room where Pam, her father, and Trent waited patiently.

"Pam dear, watch your posture"

Pam shifted her shoulders backward as her back straightened.

"Trent darling, I'm thrilled that Pamela encouraged you to dine with us. She is so into herself these days, her father and I vaguely have any idea what is happening in her world."

Trent unfolded a linen napkin, placing it on his lap. "Thank you for having me. I suggested this a while ago. I was starting the think that my Pam was ashamed of me."

Pam sensed the claw taking a dig. Since they were speaking as if she weren't in their presence, Pam wiggled around in the chair trying to maintain her upright position while keeping her elbows away from the table.

Pam's mother raised a Waterford wine glass from in front of her, positioning her perfectly manicured hand just so. "Ridiculous. How on Earth could she be ashamed of such a handsome young man? If my opinion counts, hard to come by in this small town."

Pam's father inventively smeared whipped butter across a lightly browned dinner roll. "So, Trent, what are your talents? Sports? Interested in your father's business? School?"

Pam's mother returned the crystal glass to the table. "Such pressure. Fathers are so protective."

Trent rested a silver Tiffany & Co. fork on the edge of his plate. "Some sports, football. My father's business, not so sure about that. School is good."

"Mutual interests are always healthy for a relationship." Pam's mother paused. "Pamela, are you going to engage in the conversation dear?"

Still chewing, Pam covered her mouth, feeling forced to reply. "I'm sorry. I didn't want to interrupt."

Trent lifted his fork. "Did you tell them about the audition?"

"No."

"I don't know why they even bother. Just give her the part. Where is the competition? What about you Trent? Are you auditioning as well?" Flirting, Pam's mother flicked her mascara-laden lashes.

"Without doubt. Permanent record could always look better for college," Trent lied.

"Absolutely darling. Absolutely. Thankfully, Pam's father has connections so she won't get stuck attending some dreadful community college situation, but with her grades…"

Interrupting, but cautious, Pam piped in. "What about music school?"

Giggling, Pam's mother spouted. "Silly girl."

Pam aggressively shoved away from the dining table, angrily storming across the room. Trent's eyes traced Pam moving out of the opulent dining area.

Pam's mother rolled her eyes. "Here we go."

Minding his manners, politely folding the linen napkin, Trent drew his chair from underneath the table. "Should I go check on her?"

"Yes dear. Yes, do that. Perhaps you can use some of your charm and lead her to the light."

Standing up, Trent situated the napkin on a placemat, his undertaking controlled and intentional. "I'll try my best."

The underlying tension was common within Pam's pretentious family, though they pretended as if everything was as it should be, ignoring the strain on the surface.

Pam's parents held high expectations for their only daughter. Pam, however, had a dream of her own that didn't adhere to the sophisticated checklist her family had etched in stone.

Since Trent hosted demons of his own, the exchange between Pam and her mother seemed nothing but ordinary fare. Over time, he had developed a personal set of survival skills to cope, methods that aren't always healthy for anyone involved. With few exceptions, Trent learned to numb himself to certain emotions, and his reactions to most situations were clearly a defense mechanism.

Trent found Pam outside where she sat on wooden bench tucked within the hemlocks and white roses.

"I can't believe you just embarrassed me in front of your parents! What kind of girlfriend does that?"

"I'm sorry. Barbie Botox was getting to me. She is *so* perfect you know."

"Parents are parents. What do you do? You roll with it, outsmart them. Play the game. More importantly, don't embarrass your boyfriend when he is meeting them for the first time."

Feeling constantly criticized by those closest to her, Pam rose from the bench, and began to walk away when Trent reached out, firmly grabbed her arm, and pulled her close to his wide chest. "I'm the one you can trust."

Trust? What did he mean exactly? Pam never had any reason to be untrusting of anyone. It was unclear to Pam why Trent made the comment, and yet, it was simply another example of moment where he made her feel needed—and more importantly, she felt approved of, in some odd sense.

Three

Christian was late as usual, and as I waited, I paced back and forth in front of concessions just outside the school auditorium. If I had to make one more time-killing trek to the water fountain, I would've probably pee'd in my pants right in the middle of the audition. We're not talking trickle here either; think waterfall. Besides, if I had had to go to the bathroom, I would've been too nervous to use it anyway.

Behind the two doors leading to the audition area, I heard other students confidently sharing the pieces they'd prepared for the on looking teachers.

Undeniably, my nerves were in complete control of the twitches. I was anxious, and I needed Christian for moral support. It was his idea after all. Finally, he arrived looking rushed, but if anyone was keeping track, Christian's hair was flawless. In fact, his mane appeared as if each strand was in the same place it was the day before and the day before that. He must have a photo that he spent hours every morning mimicking, that's what I thought.

"Sorry I'm late. Had to help some nerd kid in the Science hall. One of the sporties was experiencing a testosterone surge. Pick, pick, pick; that's all they do. They should all be medicated and castrated. Those genes passing down from one generation to the next must be stopped."

"Can you save the world some other day? I'm having a moment here. I don't know about this."

"Miranda, you're fine. You got this. If you don't, I will, and if I do it, neither of us will be able to show our faces in the public again. Trust me! Steel bending, dog howling, end of the world type trauma for four blocks"

Second to my Nana, Christian inspired me more than anything in the world. Their approaches were vastly different, but in the end, their encouragement and advice was warmly welcomed. I felt blessed to have their uniqueness in my cheering section.

At first glance and without knowing him, some might mistake Christian for being wispy. He appeared exceptionally pretty, and sometimes that brought about assumptions. Make no mistake though, behind that beauty, he had physical strength, an exhaustingly strong will, and absolutely no fear. Even further down, he maintained a wounded heart, and because of that, Christian suffered with a desire to be protective of everyone. No one had been there to defend him when he needed them to, so somehow, as a wall constructed around his heart, Christian secretly vowed to assist others who were made to feel insubstantial. Whether it was a conscience decision, I'm unsure, but his actions spoke from themselves.

I quit pacing when Pam and Trent cut in front of me and entered the auditorium. Beyond the daunting double doors, I caught a glimpse of the four appraising teachers sitting along the length of a long folding table near the front of the large intimidating stage. I witnessed Pam situating herself on the platform as the doors gradually shut.

Four people had auditioned before her, which had been disastrous in my evaluation. Did someone just punch me in the stomach? Was that last drink of water too much? It was vividly clear, or I should say audible to me or anyone else listening, that Pam could blow. Beautifully, she sang out filling the auditorium, spilling over into the hall.

I circled around craning my neck searching for a break in the crowded concession area, ready to bolt.

"No, no way." Grabbing my arm, Christian tilted his pretty head. "Miranda."

"You can't live through me."

"Oh yes I can. You're going. Steel Bending!" Christian warned.

"Do I even like you?"

"It's the car, I know!"

Okay, there was applause. That hadn't happened yet. Mary, Joseph, and Jesus I prayed. To the universe, I surrendered. I visually rubbed the belly of Buddha. Twisting my roite bindele, I remembered the Kabbalah's teaching and the ability of the red string to ward off misfortune. Anything. Anything! Rabbit's foot anyone? Had anyone told me to break a leg? Wait! I forgot to gargle with apple cider-honey mixture! It helped the throat right? Carbs? Did I have carbs last night? Oh, never mind that was for athletes.

Pam and Trent cracked the door, and another performer nervously sauntered towards the point of no return.

"Very good Pam."

Pam turned, peeping back into the auditorium. "Thank you Mr. Stancil."

The door closure sealed again. I was next. My stomach churned, not with butterflies, but piranhas. That damn water! As they left, I hoped that Pam and Trent might discuss the feeling in the room. They didn't, but their conversation distracted Christian from listening to the newest singer stumbling under the pressure from the eight-eyed judger.

"I wasn't flirting," Pam insisted.

"Not sure what you would call it then," Trent grunted.

Christian interjected, "Ptshh. You mind?"

Trent sneered as Christian leaned in closer to the auditorium's double doors.

"Problem?" Cocking his head, Christian gazed directly at Trent.

****

Abundant investigatory work wasn't needed for Greer to discover that Pam would be staying after school for the musical's audition. Nathan and Greer instinctively knew from the layout of the building that Pam had to pass through the main lobby of the school to leave for the day so, they set up camp and waited.

When Pam and Trent breached the corner, Nathan's arm sprung straight out to his side hitting Greer square in the chest, resulting in thud.

"Go tiger." Greer smirked.

Cleary still bent out of shape, a snarled expression owned Trent's face. Though he suspected everybody, it was obvious to Trent that Nathan was blatantly staring at what he considered his property. Nathan's mouth sagging open and his widened eyes were a dead giveaway.

"Hound dog, you want to hoist that tongue back in before I rip it from your flapper?"

"Tough guy." Greer flicked his head backward.

Nathan's arm hit Greer once more.

Greer gripped his chest. "Dude!"

Trent lunged forward toward Nathan and Greer; both shuffled in opposite directions eluding personality three.

Greer fluttered both hands. "Chill there grass glider."

Trent's attention reverted to his asset, Pam.

Nathan rested his back against a block wall. "See, he already forgot. Football helmets are not so protective after all."

Greer chuckled. "Nike strip. Swoosh."

Using two fingers, Trent gestured a motion that suggested he'd keep his eyes on Greer and Nathan. Nathan rose from the wall; his arms extended in front with his palms facing upward.

"Yo! He knows sign language even."

Greer's hand balled in a fist as he bent his elbow, lowering his arm in one quick motion. "Sweet!"

Again, Trent made a swift movement of charging the boys as Pam reached out tugging his shirtsleeve. Twisting his head while scrunching his brow, he yanked free.

"Girl!"

****

I don't remember anything. It was one complete intoxicating blur. Just the same, I didn't hear anything either since my bladder had overflowed and my ears were totally submerged underwater. I came to once I glimpsed Christian's face on the other side of the intimidating room. His aura and his hair had that effect on me, which was both calming and distracting.

"Well? Any cracked window?" I questioned.

Christian raised his brow. "Only a few over in the trailer park. Cheap glass, but other than that, nothing."

"I held back?"

"You held back."

I felt resigned. "I held back."

Christian positioned his arm on my shoulder. "Just a little. It was good. But you did it!"

"I did didn't I?"

Whatever the outcome, I listened to the calling of the universe. It wasn't so bad after all. Once I blacked out! At any rate, I did something that I had never done before. I put myself out there. How I endured the ridicule from other students would be the true test. I could always wear my floodwater pants to school to distract them from the obvious reason for taunting.

Christian was gleaming with pride as if he had gone through the process himself. In some ways, he had, well, lived through me anyway.

****

Not leaving well enough alone, Nathan and Greer trailed Trent and Pam out of the building.

"Do you think she was looking back at me?" Nathan wondered aloud.

"She was looking at you alright."

"She was?"

"Oh yeah! I expected your shirt to catch fire because the gaze was so hot. Burn a hole right through you."

"That's what I thought too."

Greer inquisitively thrusts his fingers through his hair, "Yeah, well, with all that thinking, your mind has got to be sore by now."

"What do you mean?" Nathan was lost.

"Nothing, Nathan. Nothing. That would be like squeezing the donut into the filling."

"Man, I love donuts."

****

The monster slammed the car door. "First you flirt with that old fart and next it's with those two twits!"

"Why do you always think I'm flirting with someone?"

Trent mimicked a female voice, "Thank you Mr. Stancil."

"I wasn't flirting."

"You were flirting!" Trent growled.

"What about the other two? What did I say to them?"

"Hip swaying! Hair tossing!"

"Whatever."

"Whatever! You expect me to deal with that?"

"You don't have to deal with anything."

"And you're a liar too!"

"Don't deal with it then." Pam reached for the door release.

****

The latter half of the weekend, I had sweated over nothing. So what if Pam always got the part? At least I pushed myself to the verge and entered the darkness. On a positive note, I had to thank those I included in my prayer because the blackout saved me from losing my voice the second I hit the stage, seeing as how I forgot to gargle with a miracle promising, voice clearing elixir.

I almost skipped to the school's parking lot. In my head, I was skipping like a six-year-old girl on a sidewalk who had just moved to a new neighborhood and made a new friend.

As Christian and I neared his car, we passed the rear of another car as the door shot open and Pam struggled to get out while someone held her arm from inside. I recognized the voice that scorned from the interior of the vehicle.

"You're right. I don't have to deal with anything. You had better remember that or else. You go ahead and run away. Don't think I won't tell the whole school what a dirty little whore you are. Maybe I should hook up with your mother; she'd like it."

Crying, Pam yanked free, pulling herself from Trent's car and hastily rushed to her own car parked two spots over.

I hadn't ever witnessed a couple having an argument in public before, and it was uncomfortable. They were far too young to be that serious over whatever their issues with each other might be.

Pam's car reversed into the middle of a lane then proceeded forward as her angry partner's car inched in behind.

"Something is amok in couple land," I suggested while opening the door of Christian's car.

"That's no couple. That's convenience." Christian placed a key in the ignition.

"Jenny Craig, yet another name on the waiting list." I laughed.

"Wait a minute. Script playing out in my head. No, no can't. Stop."

"Props please. One belt made out of ice cream and sadness."

"Seriously though, that guy is twisted. Since kindergarten. Twisted. In the second grade, he was always trying to kill birds on the playground."

"Hopscotch. Monkey bars. Kill birds. Pick one."

The engine roared to life.

"Seatbelt!"

Right away, I stretched for the seatbelt. Somehow, in that car, the strap always managed to get lost in the crack of the seat. Another option for muscle building, I supposed.

****

Veiled by a row of fence like bushes near the parking area, Nathan and Greer were spying on Pam until she exited the parking lot. From the distance, they hadn't heard the exchange of words between Pam and Trent.

Once Pam had vanished, Christian's car squealed in reverse out from between the two white lines. Smoke plumed in the still air, hovering above the other vehicles as the car changed direction and jolted forward.

"My sister's sister is going to kill somebody," Greer said.

"And need new tires," Nathan added.

Greer rolled his eyes. "Need new tires?"

Nathan shrugged his shoulders. "What?"

FOUR

In a dimly lit living area, Trent's father swallowed several nips of his drug of choice—vodka straight up. After several more slurps, he tilted the glass up to sky and finished the entire contents, the ice bumping his top lip. From a half-emptied bottle, he refilled a tall glass until the liquid nearly reached the rim.

Knowing her husband was thoroughly inebriated, Trent's mother, Karen, frantically scrubbed the granite counter tops with cleanser. When the front entrance of the house snapped shut, she nervously glanced upward. Karen easily made out the drunkard's slurring speech from the living room.

"Your mother wants to know how long you're going to keep lying to her?" Trent's father hammered his glass down on a coffee table causing the ice to clink the sides.

Apprehensive, Trent paced into the living area to face his daily dose of demons. "What did I lie about?"

"What did you lie about, what?"

"What did I lie about Sir?"

Karen continued spreading the cleaner, as the tension laid grips on the group of muscles running the complete span of her shoulders. The pace of her scrubbing increased, as a mother's free hand nervously trembled.

"Well, why don't we ask her?" His vodka-tainted voice boomed,

"Karen!" Lifting up the tumbler, his father topped his drink off again and took a short swig, sinking the contents just above the tops of the cubes of ice. "Karen!" He loudly summoned again.

She cringed, dropping the sponge to the countertop. Taking a deep breath, she quickly dried her hands on a hand towel. Wiping the tears from underneath her sunken eyes, Karen exited the kitchen and entered the tense room.

Following another long swig, Trent's father waved his glass at Karen, each ting of the ice wrecking her nerves.

"So you can stop driving me crazy, explain to your son here your concerns about his lies."

Karen wrung her hands together. "Really dear, it's nothing. He said he would be home at 4, and I just wondered where he was; that's all."

His father's temper flared. "Every day at four o'clock you said. More than once and quite frankly, the two of you are making my headache worse!"

In his state of mind, he wasn't making any sense, but both Trent and Karen were accustomed to the irrationality.

Trent sat on the armrest of a side chair, "It is 4:15." He knew better than to question anything.

The intoxicated man rose from the sofa and shuffled in the direction of Trent's position. Karen stepped in between them as a cautious son lifted himself from the chair's armrest.

"Let's just calm down," Karen pleaded calmly.

"I guess that fifteen minutes doesn't make it a lie? Share with your mom what was so important that fifteen minutes turned into a lie!"

"I was following my girlfriend home."

"Like you need a girlfriend," his father snarled.

"What's the big deal?"

Trent's father thrust towards Trent, and his beverage glass slipped from his hand, shattering on the ceramic tile. Vodka splashed on Trent's shoes and pooled on various sections of the flooring.

Karen screamed, "No! No!"

The broken mother was helpless trying to intervene. Once shoved to the side, resigned, Karen hopelessly slumped to the floor bawling and mumbling pleas for the scuffle to stop. There was no one to intervene as a father and a son tumbled around the cold, wet floor.

****

Not finding the whoopee cushion in her dinner chair the slightest bit amusing, Nana owed Greer one, and she had to get even. Especially, since the incident happened in a crowded public restaurant. The night it happened, Nana wanted to launch a spoonful of mash potatoes across the table, but fearing her aim was off and she might miss, Nana kept the peace. If the vegetable rocket veered slightly to the right, the large burley woman behind Greer might've come after her.

Patiently waiting at the kitchen bar with a laptop, Nana acted as normal as possible. Seconds before, she busied herself, but Nana had run out of time, and Greer was due home from school within minutes. She watched the clock on the lower toolbar of the computer, and time was up. The chatter of a school bus loaded with kids was just outside approaching an unloading point on the street.

The door entering the garage closed, causing a beep from the security box mounted on the kitchen wall. Midstream of conversation, Greer's voice echoed in the large area where two cars normally filled the space.

"She isn't going to dump that toad."

"I'm sure of it. She was looking straight at me."

With backpacks dangling from one shoulder, Nathan and Greer strolled through another door that led into the kitchen area where Nana acted nonchalant.

"Hey Nana."

Nana orchestrated a surprised expression, acting hip. "Oh, what up? What's going down?"

Nathan burst out a laugh.

Greer headed for the pantry. "Nothing much. School. This one here and his smooth self," he said, motioning to Nathan.

Greer removed a box from the pantry, reached in, retrieved two packages, and pitched one of them across the room to Nathan who caught it midair.

Suspiciously, Nana squirmed, "You two are going to ruin your appetites. It will be dinner time before you know it."

With their afternoon snack, Nathan and Greer hauled up the stairwell to Greer's room without acknowledging Nana's suggestion.

Quickly, Nana got up from the bar in order to hide the evidence. If Greer and his best friend had arrived two minutes earlier, they would have caught Nana in the act—fingerprints on the products and preparation tools in hand.

Nana scooped up the kitchen scissors and placed them in the utensil drawer. With her free hand, she snagged a piping bag off the granite countertop and began running hot water in one side of the sink.

Earlier, Nana removed the last two cream-filled snack cakes from a pantry. Delicately, like a surgeon, she separated the sealed closure with steam and removed the contents. With the talented preciseness of a pastry chef, Nana placed the tip of the piping bag in the already present hole in the side of the snack cake. Nana squeezed and transferred the content from the piping bag into to the cavity of the cream filled snack. Using a thickened sugar-water paste, she resealed the wrappers and slid them back in the box.

****

My Nana was just the cutest thing. I would never guess in a million years that she had given birth to my ultra-conservative mother. My mother must have taken after my grandfather, who passed away shortly after Greer was born.

Since my grandfather's passing, Nana had lived with us. Initially, she moved in with us to help take care of Greer and me, but since Nana was already in her early seventies, my mother thought it was best that Nana not go back to her home where she would be alone. Both my parents had full time positions to help pay for their large mortgage, so Nana's helped saved them from needing to pay for daycare. So, as it should be, home was with us.

By the time, Greer was four and I had started pre-school, my parents had converted our basement into a suite where Nana could have some semblance of privacy. Not once have I ever thought that she needed looking after. In fact, I thought that, physically, she was much more capable than my mother. My mother had let the years of babies and easy foods take a toll.

Despite her age, Nana still remained feisty. She even attended a spin class three times a week. Nana dragged my mother along, but from what I understand, mom had a hard time keeping up. Nana, who constantly joked, said that the reason my mother couldn't catch her breath was because her mouth wasn't big enough to take in the oxygen she needed. The reality of it though was that mom was out of shape, which was the reason mother's workouts were less than stellar. That and the fact that my mother had, in Nana's words, a muffin top to slow her down. I thought muffin-top put it mildly. Mom's waistline was the accumulated result of seven years on the sofa with uncountable boxes of Twinkies. As most do, mother blamed it on the fact that she had given birth to two children. For the weight to linger for fourteen years made all the sense in the world to me, I thought.

For the past month, Nana was on a quest to find true love again.

One more summer romance in the winter of her life she said. For someone who grew up without the technologies of the modern world, Nana surfed the World Wide Web like a fourteen-year-old. She was acquainted with and used Twitter, Facebook, Pinterest, and totally blowing my mind was her obsession with iTunes. Now, she was making use of internet dating sites, swearing it was easier than shopping for a loaf of bread at the grocer.

Watching someone in the January of her life searching for Mr. Right was quite admirable and adorable.

When Christian and I returned from school, we discovered Nana searching away.

“Hey Nana. Any luck in the hunt?”

“So many to choose from. What do you think about this guy?”

I glanced over a profile. “Don’t know if he can compete with you.”

Nana swiveled around on her stool, “How are my two favorite people doing today? Oh yeah, speaking of competition, how did the audition go?”

Christian planted himself on a barstool next to Nana. “Ms. Nana, she was amazing.”

I searched the refrigerator. “Would you stop?”

“No seriously. I couldn’t have done it better myself.”

Nana giggled, raising her brow; she had heard Christian sing before. “No you couldn’t. Miranda is not one to sing her own tributes. Her parents, God love them, but they’re overly humbled, and I think that has rubbed off on at least one their children. That other one, still not sure about him.”

“Nana you’re sweet, but there is still one huge obstacle.”

Christian snatched a pan from an overhead pothook. “The cooking spray.”

“The cooking spray?” Nana questioned.

"He is talking about P-a-m, Pam."

"Popular girl?" Nana asked.

"In her own mind, I say." Christian made a motion of banging the pan he held on his head.

"Christian, we have to face facts. She is pretty, popular, and no doubt, she can sing. You heard her. If her parents bought off the staff, well..."

"True, but I don't even think the judges hear her voice. Something about that look puts them all in a trance."

"Now that I think about it, she resembles one of those shimmering vampires."

"Miranda, she has been trained since birth. The walk. The flirt and the alluring giggle. You've seen her mother. Identical."

"Ah, one of those girls. Believe it or not, and even though I'm as old as the stones of the Wailing Wall, we had that same girl in my day."

Giving Nana my attention, I seated myself next to Christian. "Did she live the dream? Find her Ken and live happily ever after?"

"It was the sixties, and I think she ended up a hippy or something. Pot smoking flower girl. The chief, uh, brownies made her fat too. Last I heard, she was trailing across country with some longhaired freak following around a group called The Mamas and The Papas. I doubt you youngsters have ever heard of them."

Distracting our conversation, from upstairs, we heard screams of desperation.

Nana grinned. "Wasabi."

The thumping on the bathroom floor, the swoosh of water churning through the pipes, and the male driven "Ugggh" triggered Christian and me to an uncontrollable cackle.

"Nana, where do you get such ideas?"

Nana's face turned reflective and serious. "I'm going to throw this out there." She paused. "Why are the two of you not boyfriend and girlfriend?"

How could we not laugh harder? First, Nana mentioned brownies baked with marijuana, then suddenly Greer and Nathan were wailing, and now she revealed an outlandish speculation about Christian and me.

"What's so funny about that? Not a day goes by that the two of you are not together. It's an obvious next step."

I wondered, "What about Greer and Nathan?"

Nana winced, "Oh no, no, no they'd have ugly babies."

FIVE

Soon after the scuffle was over, Trent's father lay slumped over the arm of the sofa. Next to him rested a large empty bottle of vodka and a tumbler holding only slowly melting ice cubes.

Karen's hands trembled as she picked up the last small chards of glass off the cold tile. Hearing an exterior door close, she lifted herself heading to the window where she peeled back the curtain. Outside, Trent's car withdrew from the driveway with the lights off. As the pressure built around her eyes, Karen let the curtain fall back in place as she hid her face with her hands and sobbed.

Karen had finally reached her limit. Twenty years in a mentally abusive marriage and ten years with a practicing alcoholic had pushed her so far that Karen's condition resembled someone with post-traumatic stress disorder. The only thing missing was exploding IEDs, gunfire, and dead bodies. However, the emotional and physical wounds were evident.

****

After wasting fourteen gallons of tap water, Greer and Nathan managed to quell the flames that flickered on the tips of their tongues. Greer quickly transitioned into retaliation mode after his two-time tangle with wasabi paste. Hunching over the counter in the bathroom, Greer directed Nathan regarding the scissors and a stack of paper cups.

"Cut it about one inch from the bottom."

Nathan examined the paper cup. “Dude, do you have a ruler? How much is one inch?”

“Dude, seriously? We’re in the bathroom. You should be very familiar with what one-inch looks like. There’s not going to be a grade for technical difficulty.”

“Technical what?”

Once the materials were ready, Nathan and Greer left the bathroom and tiptoed down the hall. Passing the thermostat, Greer maneuvered a lever to the heat position and slid the gauge up high.

****

That wasn’t the first time that Nana had brought up the idea about Christian and I being a couple. True, we *were* together all the time. True, we *were* compatible as they come. Whatever chemistry was involved in attracting two people together causing them lock lips, press bodies together, and discard clothing, well, we didn’t have that. If anything, we were more like close siblings, like twins. The relationship between twins seemed to transcend the typical brother sister relationship. Besides, Christian would never break up with his car. Not for me and from what details I know, I suspected that he wouldn’t end that romance for anyone. For him, it wasn’t worth it. Unless someone had a four hundred something engine under the hood, then there might’ve been the slightest chance for negotiations.

As I turned in for the night, the audition lived in the forefront of my thoughts. Not because I thought I had a chance, but because I felt that they might’ve considered me for some other role in the musical. I mean, not everyone in show biz is a Barbie girl right? Even if it meant I had to wear silver duct tape across my mouth. Though I don’t recall any members of The Go Go’s having a clamped mouths during their performances. What about the drummer, did she sing? I should have learned to play drums.

Stressing out about the situation was making me hot. Surely, I'm too young for high blood pressure. Menopause? No, not yet. Suddenly, I shouted loud enough for the entire house to hear. "I'm going to kill somebody!"

They must've turned the heat on. It was a clever move. Therefore, Greer was one up on the scoreboard. As I said, Greer was very sneaky with his tricks, and they often appeared when least expected.

Sitting on my bed with my laptop, I pressed the button on the fan remote, and then, there was no escaping the avalanche. When the blades of the ceiling fan picked up speed, twenty paper cups flew off the blade letting loose an indoor rainstorm. I owed him one.

I was soaked, and my bed was wet, but luckily, my laptop was fine. That would be bad news for an internet addict. Bad news for Greer too, because I'd be forced to slip razor blades in his bed sheets. I'm not sure how long I pleaded for a laptop, but unlike the Sesame Street backpack, my parents thought the computer might help me be more successful in school. How so, was one more question added to list of things I can't answer, but if that was what they believed, then it worked for me.

****

As soon as her parents were tucked away for the night, Pam carefully crawled out of her bottom floor bedroom window. Upset, Trent had phoned her earlier persuading Pam to sneak out for the night because he needed someone to talk to about what happened with his father. The excuse was just a ploy, but personality one got his way.

With the lights off, his car rolled to a stop at the end of a driveway where Pam was waiting. Pam opened the closure, sat down inside, and shut the door quietly. In light of the fact that Pam's house was enormous, no one would have heard a door slamming anyway.

Trent's foot eased down on the accelerator resuming the car's movement to a slow pace down the street. Five houses away from

Pam's residence, he flipped on the headlights. Increasing the speed of the car, Trent reached for Pam's hand.

Seeming sincere, he spoke. "You're not mad at me are you?"

"Not anymore. So, what happened with your dad?"

"Making sure you got home made me late, and my dad went ballistic." Since it's late, the monster's eye was barely open; he prodded but spoke softly.

There was no need for her boyfriend to follow Pam home; she knew that, but she apologized anyway. Pam enjoyed this gentle side, this little boy that needed affection.

"I'm sorry."

"Can we hang at the park?" Trent asked tenderly.

"It's late."

"Please? If you care?"

The park was empty and dark where the sleepy-eyed monster placed the gear in park and shut off the ignition.

Trent positioned his other hand on top of Pam's, which rested softly in her lap as he leaned in. Pam reciprocated as their lips met midway. He shifted his body so that it was facing Pam, and he drew himself closer. One hand eased behind Pam's head, underneath her hair. His resting hand inched up the center part of her blouse searching for a top button. Pam reached, grasping his roaming appendage. Becoming aggressive, Trent hastily veered Pam's protective hand away. She reached once more.

Somewhere behind the parked car, an automobile engine grumbled in the darkness, the exhaust drumming a heavy sound. Trent continued his pursuit, but Pam resisted.

Distracting a predator and its prey, blinding headlights beamed through the rear window of Trent's car. The engine boomed louder, and spontaneously, the blinding car commenced circling around in three-sixties. One after the other for several minutes.

Trent and Pam turned, staring out of the rear window, as the bright lights sporadically flashed across their expressionless faces, causing their eyes to squint in intervals. All they could see were flashes of red and white between plumes of smoke. The car ceased moving, and the headlights pierced through the rear window of Trent's parked car, blinding the two. Like Stephen King's *Christine*, the car seemed to have awareness of a boy seeking to have his way with a girl.

Not knowing what else to do, Trent ignited his own car's engine and pulled away, steering clear of the midnight maniac. Once Trent's car reached the far side of the parking lot, the mystery car shut its lights, leaving nothing but the glow of two red taillights leaving the dark scene.

Minutes later, Pam reclaimed her room through the window.

When Trent arrived home, he slipped into his house undetected and went straight to bed. In a different room, Karen shut a book, turned off a pale reading lamp, and closed her eyes, relieved that her son was home safe.

****

Miranda's mother struggled to keep pace with the strenuous workout routine. Nana did just fine and even had enough energy to encourage her overweight daughter.

"Come on! I am twenty-five years older than you are! Got to look my best for my hot date!"

Miranda's mother sighed. "Mother really."

"Really nothing. If you want to curl up on the sofa, cocoon, and turn into a blueberry muffin, you go for it."

"I can't breathe."

"Your mouth is too small."

"Mother."

"I want to keep my butt flab free for my sexy man."

"How embarrassing. Mother really."

"Embarrassing? You don't think that you're embarrassing yourself with those cottage cheese thighs?"

"Mother I gave birth. Two children remember? I can't help it."

"What you can't help is shoving donuts in your mouth."

"Mother I think you've forgotten that having babies wreaks havoc on the body."

"I think you have forgotten that you last gave birth fourteen years ago, and you don't still have something inside of you needing to feed, but you're feeding for three."

****

Another average morning of high school had begun. As expected, Nathan and Greer waited in the corridor near the front of the school. Convinced that Pam was engaging with him, it became necessary for Nathan to be vigilant in his quest to get the girl.

Due to a late one the night before, Pam was nearly tardy for homeroom. Nathan and Greer had minutes before the warning bell too, and they would use each second waiting for Pam.

Not looking altogether, Pam arrived rushing through the main entrance of the school.

"Whoa, your girlfriend had a rough night."

Nathan grinned. "Wish it was rough with me."

"It would be," Greer said jokingly.

As Pam hurried past the two, Nathan's arm shifted and pegged Greer in the side.

Greer grunted. "They have medication for that you know."

"Did you see that? She looked right at me."

Greer placed his hand on his forehead, "Of course she did."

"Just a matter of time." Nathan beamed.

"In another time even." Greer stroked his forehead.

"What?"

Greer drew a fist and lightly knocked on Nathan's head. "Are you in there? Hello?"

****

It was quiz day, and class was about to begin. Thanks to my brother and his water torpedoes, I used my last twenty minutes before bedtime changing bed clothing instead of reviewing the test material. Christian plopped down in the desk in front of me as I scanned my notes from the weeklong lectures.

"Just get me through this. Did you study?" Christian exhaled.

"No, my social calendar was filled. Yes, I did. I studied over the weekend. I tried last night, but weasel face tried to drown me. Did you study?"

"Uh, no. Why bother? It's all bogus. Just about the time our spot on the sofa is properly sunken in, there will be some new revelation that the teachings of today are incorrect. I can read. I can add. I get the basics of gravity and understand all the basic functions of a PC. What more is there to know? How many phones and computers have you had? You know how it works. The minute you master it, something new comes along, and it takes hours to read the owner's manual that only Bill Gates understands. When the owners' manual starts to makes sense to the normal folk, months and months later, they change the damn operating system. It's just too much."

"As long as you have a plan."

Christian winced, "Plan? What plan? One delicious day at a time. Oh, oh, I got distracted. Who is Devin Walters?"

"Got me." My curiosity peaked, I closed my notebook.

"You haven't seen it have you?"

Dammit! I hate it when that happens. Just as Christian was about to dish, the bell chimed. Test time.

Christian shifted around in his desk. "Shit."

How might I concentrate on bubbling in the ovals on the answer sheet while wondering about this Devin Walters? What had I not seen? Had he tried to save another person from the pain and anxiety of the teenaged world earlier in the morning?

****

Miranda's mother made it through the workout. By the end of the session, she was sweating profusely and clutching the walls to help her move along while she rapidly drew breath from the air.

Nana was still energized by the time they reached the hair salon. Longing for a donut and a soda, Miranda's mother crept to a chair and plopped down like a rag doll.

After numerous searches, online chats, and checking off a strict checklist of pros and cons, Nana had met someone that she deemed appropriate to go out on a date with. She had already shopped and found a sexy, age-appropriate dress, and the last thing left was a hair color tune-up and a trim.

The hairdresser brushed hair dye on a clump of Nana's hair. "Well, good for you, girl."

Nana smiled. "And he is so sexy, many years younger."

Nana's daughter grew embarrassed. "Mother!"

"We should take this hair up a notch then," the hairdresser suggested.

A synthetically implanted twenty-something hot tart strolled in front of Nana. Using both hands, Nana lifted her boobs upward. "Do you have a forklift?"

"Mother!"

"Girl, we can do whatever you want. Paint it, pluck it, wrap it, and tuck it."

"Fix up it; that handsome man might fu…"

Interrupting, Miranda's mother gasped. "MOTHER!"

Nana waved one hand. "Calm down, and stop calling me mother."

Stepping backwards, the hairdresser stared. "Girl, you are a livewire for sure. Who could hold a candle to you?"

****

Of all days to have a test with trick questions, it had to be the day that Christian left me with a cliffhanger. I felt like I'd blackened in two hundred circles, though the test was only fifty questions.

I noticed that Christian finished long before I did. Most likely, he closed his eyes and randomly picked a letter. He did that once before and had to do time in summer school. He looked like an idiot considering that particular test had trick questions, and he answered that one plus two equaled twelve. I guessed that could be correct depending on one's prospective of the world. Christian definitely argued that point with the school counselor as he tried to escape his summer sentence. The counselor wanted Christian to explain the other seventy incorrect answers, and Christian went on to tell the guy that most of history was hearsay, that most of it couldn't be proven beyond the recounts of some person who wrote it in a book. The counselor scoffed when Christian suggested it was up to him to prove that Christian's answer choices that were marked wrong were actually wrong.

Never once did it dawn on me what Christian was keeping from me. Something to do with someone named Devon, and whatever the secret was, it suddenly needed to be a surprise.

After class, Christian guided me down the hallway with his hands masking my eyes.

"Are you about to push me over the edge?" I asked.

"Well, then you won't have to jump."

"You're too kind."

"I try. Are you ready?"

Reaching up, I gripped his forearms, "Just push. Don't tell me when you're going to do it."

Christian removed his hands. I stood facing a wall where the audition results were positioned in the center of a bulletin board.

"Shit." I was in shock.

"Now, we need to arrange a kidnapping," Christian seriously stated.

"Who is Devin Walters?"

"Exactly. Obviously we need to keep closer tabs on the social order around here."

I lightly shoved Christian. "If he were in the social order I'd think we'd know who he is."

"Well, anyway, back to the kidnapping." Can you believe it? I had no doubts."

"What? You had no doubt that I would be the understudy of a cooking spray?"

Christian's brow flicked. "I know, I know, we can slip some tiny pieces of glass in her diet drink."

"Does this mean I have to follow her around?" I questioned.

"You'll be the closet to the diet drink."

So there it was. No surprises that Pam got the lead, though it was shocking that I had been chosen to understudy in the event of her demise. Christian was well into the planning stages of conjuring up that event. Glass, snakes, abductions, or whatever else needed to go down.

Keeping in mind that Christian was completely OCD, he jokingly prepared a checklist as we walked to his car after school.

"So, we're going to need some rope, duct tape, and a body bag."

"I bet her boyfriend has some in the back of his car."

"No thanks. They probably used it in some physical situation. Gross."

I reached for the door handle, "What the hell?" Something greasy lingered on the underside. "That is disgusting." I said.

"You're telling me."

"No, something is on your door handle."

Christian hurried to the passenger side of the car, "No way. If someone messed with my car…"

****

Nathan and Greer scurried to a grassy area behind a fence near the parking lot just in time to get out of Miranda and Christian's sights.

Greer squatted to the ground. "Look at her face."

Nathan kneeled alongside. "Oh crap. Look at your sister's face. He is p-o'd."

Nathan and Greer spied as Christian frantically circled around his car looking for obvious signs of tampering. After finding nothing, Christian and Miranda entered the car and backed away.

"Check it; here he goes," Greer whispered.

"You are a dead man if he catches wind of this."

"I'm not worried. He wouldn't ever mess up his hair."

****

Old cars have issues. They leak, they rattle, and the interiors maintain a distinctive odor. I thought door handles, operation wise, were relatively simple, but Christian explained that moving parts needed lubricating on occasion. Apparently, grease was oozing out from inside the opening mechanism of the door.

As we waited for the long line of cars to inch forward so we could get out of the school parking area, Christian checked his hair in the rearview mirror with his typical routine.

"Uh oh, the FBI is on to us. What is this car doing?"

I pivoted and look through the rear window. The car in behind us was weaving from one side to the other. A Few seconds passed and the car's lights started flashing, and the driver tooted the horn.

At first, I assumed something was wrong, which prompted the warning. However, Christian jumped the gun and went straight to the conclusion that the person attempting to get our attention was an asshole because they were trying to get out the parking lot faster. But as Christian's slowed to a stop, the car and the a-hole slowly pulled along my side of the car. Hoping that no liquids had seeped out of the gears, I reached for the crank and rolled down the window. No automatic switches here. Again, with the muscles, I thought as I strained to wind the old window down as it cracked and rattled.

The driver had a doll face, immediately reminding me of the actor James Dean with a slight touch of the singer John Mayer. His hair was light brown, shiny, and tossed about on top. When he spoke, his teeth gleamed with white, and his eyes brightened up with every word. As if his teeth weren't enough to garner my attention, his puffy lips rhythmically matched the tone of his wording.

"Hey, there is paint coming off your tires."

Before the hunk finished the word tire, Christian whirled out of the muscle maker. Not knowing what else to do, I got out as well. Christian was already reacting with several words that I wouldn't repeat in front of the alluring stranger who was kind enough to inform us about the decorative pattern on the pavement.

Baffled, the person who alerted us of the fiasco stared as Christian threw a kindergarten type temper tantrum.

"He'll be okay. Thanks."

"No worries," Mr. Mysterious lips turned up.

****

Laughing hysterically from their location on the grassy knoll,

Nathan and Greer absorbed the action playing in front them.

"If he finds out, he is going to kill us."

Nathan pointed in Christian's direction. "Not if he explodes first. Look, I think he is going to cry."

"Big baby," Nathan choked out with a laugh.

With some clever persuading, Greer and Nathan had convinced a couple of teachers that they needed to leave class early that afternoon to get a book from the media center for a very important homework assignment. They met up just outside of school armed with strategic plan. With limited time to waste, the two managed to wedge numerous paintball bullets on each tire of the red classic. When Christian pulled away, the tires turning left behind trails of paint dots marking the parking lot.

****

I had my suspicions about who set up the prank. If I was correct, it would have been the first time that Greer pulled off something outside of our house. Never before had he pinpointed Christian for attack, but then it might not have been Greer at all. Christian was a moving target for passive bullying. Small things had happened before, usually to his locker. Since Christian was confident and buff, he was mostly safe from the usual cowards that typically confront someone in a situation where it's more one on one.

Although there was a slight diversion in our typical after school activities, I arrived home before Nana finished getting ready for her date. I was so happy that Nana has found someone with common interest. I had some exciting news for her too.

I knocked on Nana's door.

"Come in."

Nana looked fantastic, and with her new dress that flattered her figure, and with her vamped up hair color, she appeared ten years younger.

"Nana, wow! You could be my mother."

"Not tonight dear. Tonight I'm a...what do they call that?" Nana paused. "Tonight, I'm a cougar."

I couldn't help but laugh; she was so cute. "So guess what?"

"You and Christian decided to take the next step?"

"Hardly. Not Christian. Besides he would never break up with his car."

"Ridiculous. So what else could it be?" Nana thought as her eyes widened. "You got the part!"

"Yes and no. I'm going to understudy."

"That's great news." Nana was genuinely excited.

I sat down on the edge of an armchair. "Not so sure myself. I'm not cut out for stuff like this."

"Nonsense. Miranda dear, if I could leave you with any advice, I would tell you that though the road seems long, curvy, and full of potholes, the truth is that the path is short, and no matter what the obstacles, the conclusion is the same for everyone. A dead end. So do your best navigating, and don't take things too serious. Each moment shall pass. Took me many years to relax. Not that I'd condone it, but I should've eaten the brownies."

There was a knock at her bedroom door.

"Come in."

My mother stepped through the doorway. "Mother he is here."

Nana launched a paw in front of her. "Grrr, time to prowl."

"MOTHER!"

"Go get 'em Nana."

Nana turned serious. "Now, when we get to the living room, I'm introducing the two of you as my sisters." Nana pointed at me, "You're going to be my younger sister," She pointed at my mother. "You're going to be my older sister."

"Mother really!"

"Why do you keep calling me Mother?" Nana snickered.

I trailed Nana and her handsome date out the front door. So far, I was impressed with Nana's choice and even more so when he opened the rear door of car for her. As Nana's date entered the backseat on the opposite side, he smiled and waved at me. The fact that he had a driver to cart them around was even more impressive. He earned points for that.

When the town car reversed out of the drive, I caught a glimpse of their driver. Like a nudge from the universe, I recognized the person in charge of their transportation. I found him just adorable then as I had earlier that day.

Six

When I escaped my bedroom the next morning, the evidence of Greer's handy work smashed me in the face. Literally. At some point during the night hours, Greer skillfully wrapped and sealed the opening of my bedroom door with plastic wrap. Since I was half-asleep trying to get to the bathroom, I walked right into his creative trap.

Greer abandoned his bedroom just as I began battling with the plastic wrap entanglement.

"You look like a movie star."

When I swung out to grab him, I tumbled to the carpet since the strands of plastic had latched onto my legs.

"Whatsahappening," Greer spouted intentionally making it sound as though he were trying to say wasabi. I managed to stretch out and snatch one of his shoestrings, hanging on, and Greer crashed into the wall. Then he joined me on the hallway floor. Mom thumped up the stairwell, immediately assuming her role as parent and peacekeeper.

"You two are brother and sister. You shouldn't be fighting like this. This has got to stop."

With that motivating speech, we were convinced to stop fighting forever more. NOT! Whenever mom comes around, Greer always turns into her little helpless baby. This tough guy scrunches up his face just right as his shoulders slump a little to further his sympathetic response.

"She started it."

I started it? I was in bed. I learned not to say anything. Remaining quiet seemed to take me out of the lecture equation. Every time Greer said anything, the noose would tighten around his neck little by little.

"I don't care who started it. Now, clean this mess up. Greer, you're going to miss the bus. If you do, you're grounded."

"Mom," he whined.

"Get out of this house and catch the bus."

And I remained uninvolved where Greer was threatened with a grounding for doing something totally unrelated to the battle in the hallway. Silence works.

He knew better than to pull that baby boy crap around dad because dad would have him out in the driveway underneath the car changing to oil teaching him how to be a man. Certainly, the ability to master a socket wrench meant that manhood status was an eventuality.

****

Eating breakfast, I waited for Christian to pick me up for school, looking out the widow only twice, as if my hearing had stopped working overnight.

Nana strolled through dressed in full-blown workout gear heading to the fridge for orange juice.

"Morning Nana. How was your hot date?"

"It was wonderful. Got to get to the gym and work off the dinner calories. You know I'm not afraid to eat. My only fear is the clumps that collect where we'd rather not have them."

"I hear you. The two indentions in the sofa should be proof enough for some people."

"So, are you excited about rehearsal?" Nana sipped on the orange juice.

"Not so much."

"Let me ask you this. Why are you doing it then?"

"I love to sing. I want to perform. It's my dream. I just don't like the idea of walking in the shadow of the most popular girl in school."

"Then focus on your dream, your goals. Don't linger so much on the hurdles. The hurdles always seem larger than they truly are. If you use your energy tuned into the obstacles, those challenges tend to expand."

"Or I could go with Christian's plan. It involves duct tape and kidnapping."

Nana chuckled. "That might work too."

I heard an engine rumbling from two streets over.

"Time to go. Thanks for the advice Nana. Try not to kill mother at the gym."

"She'll be winded by the time she comes down from upstairs. That walk from the master bath to the landing is pure hell, you know. Worse than the hiking through the Grand Canyon."

****

As they did every day, Nathan and Greer were hanging out prior to school starting. Devin Walters crossed their paths in the narrow corridor.

"Whoa, I didn't know James Dean goes to school here."

Clueless, Nathan questioned, "James who?"

"Rebel Without a Cause, Giant. You know, James Dean."

"Never heard of him. He must be new here."

"So anyway, Miranda looked like a complete noodle. I got to keep my eyes open. I'm sure that somewhere, somehow she will pull something big."

"I think you need to lighten up on your sister and stop it with the pranks."

"Why would I want to do that? That's what sisters are for. She wears big girl pants. She can take care of herself."

"No, hear me out. See, your sister is the link to get us closer to Pam."

"Do you ever think of anything else?"

"Like what?"

Greer motioned into the air. "Like that." A school bell chimed.

"Dude!" Nathan shuffled a backpack to his shoulder.

****

Miranda's mother lay collapsed on the floor as several people hovered overhead fanning her face. The extreme workout had gotten the best of her, either that, or she never fully recovered from hiking from the master bathroom to the kitchen.

"Can you even make it through the grocery store without getting winded and needing to call 911?" Nana prodded.

"Mother, I'm dying and you're joking about it."

"You're right. I'm sorry. I'll be right back."

With her daughter left lying on the gym floor, Nana rushed from the gym to the business next door.

Two trainers lifted Miranda's mother off the floor and guided her demanding body to a seating area. "I'll get you some water," one trainer said, stepping away.

"Thanks."

Seconds later, the trainer revisited with the water at about the time Nana returned from next door. "You're probably dehydrated. Drink some of this it will help you feel better."

Nana moved in closer, "I know what will help you."

"What Mother?"

"This." Casually, Nana hurled a bag of donuts into her daughter's lap. "In three minutes you'll be as good as new."

****

I inhaled a long, slow deep breath trying to remain conscious. A week had gone by since the announcement on the bulletin board and the time for musical rehearsals had arrived. Hesitantly, I entered into the sizable auditorium unsure of what to do, where to go, or how these things work exactly since I'd never been involved in anything like this before.

I eased down in a chair closest to the stage when he padded across the platform where he sat down on a stool at a piano positioned near the left side. That had to be him, Devin Walters. The guy in the parking lot. The guy transporting Nana and her date. They guy whose name Christian and I had never heard circling around in the social gossip.

When Devin hit the first few notes on the piano, I caught a chill. Maybe it was the way he slowly closed his eyes and dissolved into the music that caused the sensation. He was amazing. Or my hormones were reacting to the gentle sounds seething from the left side of the auditorium.

Breaking my stare and concentration, Pam's singing broadcast outward from the opposite side of the stage. There was nothing new about her; I hadn't even noticed her standing there. I tried to resist rolling my eyes, but I did it anyway.

Next, my eyes scanned the room seeking an unattended diet soda can that might belong to Pam. Maybe Christian had the right idea. Where can I find tiny fragments of glass? Ah ha, there was crash on 23rd street the other day, so there must be remnants of shattered glass at the scene.

I studied the sheet music as Devin was playing. Unbelievably, I still understood the notes even though I hadn't been involved in orchestra or band in years. I memorized the words as they came and recognized that Pam was hitting every scheduled note change like a pro. Maybe the truth was that she didn't sound all that great. Maybe it was her magical powers of seduction, the gift of being a vampire. One bite just below the ear, a willing neck, left to spend eternity mesmerizing the judges, and boys, and everyone. Through elementary school. Through high school. Through endless college nights, hypnotically luring everyone within an earshot. Never mind the glass; I needed a sliver bullet and a dagger. It wouldn't be as easy as shoving her out into the sunlight since apparently that trick didn't work anymore for those working as vampire slayers. Now, vampires were glistening. They were in love and were pretty. Modern day vamps possessed insurmountable sums of cash for flashy cars and glass houses. They spent summer vacation on private islands in Brazil then returned in the fall for school where they attended for consecutive years and no one seems to notice.

****

With rehearsals underway, Nathan and Greer implemented their latest strategy to get closer to Pam. Just beyond the closed doors of the auditorium, Pam sang remarkably, and the two best friends recognized her voice. Though he was already in a trance, Nathan attempted to persuade Greer in engaging with Miranda in a normal conversation.

"Why would that be suspicious?" Nathan scooted closer to the door.

"Oh, I don't know. Maybe because I never ask my sister anything."

"Think of something. Maybe you need a ride home?"

"Me in the car with that hair product wearing junkie lunatic? Not happening. She won't talk to Pam for us, especially me. Besides, she already tried to get me grounded this morning for doing nothing. There's no way she'll do me a favor."

Nathan cupped his ear against the door. "What could I ask her then?"

"Maybe you could find out if my sister's sister needs new tires yet," Greer suggested.

"Like that's a good question."

"You think of something then."

"Why do I have to do everything?"

"Oh I don't know, because you're the one with the tongue hanging out his mouth."

Seven

I refrained from blacking out during rehearsals. It was easy enough since I didn't really do anything but watch and listen. Not sure what I expected for the first day, really. In my imagination, I pictured myself standing behind Pam, mimicking her motions or something along those lines. There was no life in that room except for Mr. Stancil who seemed to get fired up for the craziest reasons. He sure loved his creation, no doubt; his passion was obvious, but whatever he was doing with his fingers was over the top. Damn those jazz hands.

I was surprised that she still remembered my name when Pam spoke to me while everyone was exiting the auditorium. She was sincere it seemed even if I felt very uneasy responding to her questions. I kept in mind that she had powers and I wasn't wearing a garlic necklace. The next time we rehearsed, I mentally noted to wear my half of a friendship pendant since Christian swears it is magical—he said so back in elementary school. I could rub some garlic on it for an added element of protection. Did that still work? Had that theory been cast aside in the twilight of a new moon during an eclipse just before breaking dawn?

The uneasiness increased when my weasel brother and his sidekick appeared at my side like the kinds of pesky flies that hover around horse farms.

"What are you two doing here?"

I couldn't imagine why they were talking to me, and it had to be a set-up for some prank, I was sure.

Shyly, Nathan asked, "Does your sister need new tires?"

Greer's arm jolted upward and nailed Nathan.

What else was I to think? "Are you two high? I don't have a sister."

I hadn't seen his face, but I detected the scent with hints of sandalwood, vanilla, and a dusting of clove. It suddenly became a weird moment, for sure. Nathan, Greer, Pam, and now Devin Walters all circled around me in the same room. Maybe they were all descendants of Vladislaus Dracula, and they were sizing me up for an afternoon snack.

"Hey guys. Good rehearsal," Devin praised.

His voiced still sounded as pleasant as it had in the parking area. If Devin's voice was a cake, I would refer to it as red velvet. Now, I might fade-out.

I glanced behind me, looking for the doors in case I needed to get out of there quickly before I slid down the dark tunnel. The auditorium doors opened, and making things even more bizarre, Trent walked through. His face appeared as though he had been eating sour patch kids, and I noticed that, rapidly, Pam's demeanor shifted as she urgently gathered her stuff together. I was right; there was troubled waters on lovers' lane. It was obvious to me more than ever because from afar, before I stepped into this realm of possibility, they seemed so together.

"I've got to run guys. It was fun. I'll see you next time." Pam nervously backed away.

Greer raised his shoulders. "Well, I guess we should get going too."

"Uh, yeah. Later Miranda. See ya James."

Greer set his arm free and whacked Nathan across the chest. I still don't know what they wanted, but they split before I asked. Still, with those two, it was probably something ridiculous. They had eaten the brownies. All of them.

"Sorry about that. My brother and his friend are stoned, or maybe they're just stupid. I'm not sure which."

Devin lifted his hand. "I'm Devin by the way."

I did the same, and our hands met. "Miranda."

His skin was just a velvety. That made me nervous. And those eyes…

"Did your boyfriend's car turn out okay?"

"Who? Oh. Yeah, it was fine. Christian's a freak when it comes to his car."

"It's a nice car. Not my thing, but to each his own I suppose."

Inside I was screaming, "Yay, we've got something in common." Please, Buddha and the gang don't let this prince mention anything involving four-hundred and blah blah.

****

Hurried, Nathan and Greer shoved both double doors of the auditorium open where Christian was just about to enter as the boys whizzed through.

"Gummy Worms. Ease up on the sugar!"

Nathan and Greer didn't even acknowledge him because they were pinpointing where to place the blame since their plan had failed.

"Dude, you blew our chance," Nathan expressed.

"I blew it? Pop quiz. Do you ever hear anything that comes out of your mouth?"

"I tried to get you to ask the questions."

****

Any other time, this situation would have left me speechless. I'm not good at making small talk. Lucky for me, the universe arranged the planets just perfect allowing a connection between two people that Devin and I both knew. A second thing we had in common. Point being, since I lacked the art of summoning a creative conversation that gives me something to discuss with Devin.

"No, I'm not a paid driver. That's my grandfather. I just do it for fun, and he enjoys having me around."

"Nice. My grandmother seemed to have a good time."

Devin grinned. "She is so much fun."

"Yeah, Nana is a riot."

Since I was enjoying the conversation, I forgot all about Christian picking me up until I noticed him strutting down the center aisle of the auditorium.

"So, I guess I will see you around? My personal driver has arrived."

"Your boyfriend?"

"No. No boyfriend."

"I look forward to it."

Oh God I'm dying. He was looking forward to it? The way he said "your boyfriend" was almost as if he knew better. Or was it a kind of questioned confirmation? He did mention it twice. Like a little girl, with sidewalk chalk in hand, I think I skipped up the aisle to meet Christian.

"Devin?" Christian asked, figuring who else it could be.

"That's Devin." I answered.

"He is sure to shake things up around this dreadful minefield. What's his resume read like?"

"Not sure about the details. He just moved to town. He came over and introduced himself, asked me about your car, and called you my boyfriend."

"People and their assumptions."

"Don't worry. I assured him that your affairs are strictly limited to your car."

Christian scoffed, "Thanks for that." Sarcastically he went on, "He is going to cause a catfight."

"Catfight?"

"Get with it Chickie. I already know the entire chapter one. An easy chapter, I must say."

I was confused. "Have you been outside with Greer and Nathan toasting your brain cells?"

"With those two cheese crackers? Hardly."

"So, what chapter are you talking about?"

"Trust me. The words might have been invisible, but heartbreaker was written on both of his shirtsleeves. That look was put together with an agenda."

"Seems nice enough."

"Of course he does. That's covered on page one. Be nice straight out of the gate."

"Who is having a catfight?"

"Have you actually ever looked at the faces of these farm breeders around here? First, I am taken, as you know. Second, these girls around her will be dumbstruck with a new boy around that actually knows how to comb his hair, wears shoes that are not made for trumping through cow shit, and owns a shirt that is not multi-purpose. School, church, grocery store, and last but not least, a funeral service."

"Don't hold back."

"I don't discriminate."

"You forgot something," I said.

"What's that?"

"He can formulate sentences using real words without referring to someone as dawg or shawty."

"True dat, yo."

On the way back to the car, I informed Christian on the exact specifics of our first rehearsal for "Whole World Lost Its Head." He agreed with me that it was a brilliant concept. The whole theme of the musical geared around a female rock star and a well-known saying "Be careful what you ask for because you just might get it."

I knew something was up when I saw Trent's sourpuss expression minutes before. It seems like destiny that Christian and I once again stumbled upon a couple's drama where the macho football player was blocking Pam as she squirmed to get to her car.

"Would you just let me go! Why are you doing this?"

"You're the one doing this!"

"Am I not supposed to talk to anyone ever?"

"Flirt. You mean flirt. Always flirting," Trent barked.

"Please just let me leave."

Trent detected the two of us, and then he broke his advance, but as Pam reached the car and placed a key in the lock, Trent pushed, pressing her tightly against the cold metal.

"You run! Like you always do!"

"You're hurting me."

Booming across the lot, Christian bellowed protectively, "HEY!"

Trent receded from Pam, and she hastily slipped inside the driver's compartment. The monster's sleepy eye fully open, he shot Christian a look that could kill, but then he pivoted to his own car. When Trent was out of sight, Christian checked his life partner for signs of sabotage.

"That guy. I'm telling you he is trouble."

Shocked, I questioned, "What's she thinking?"

"That's going to end badly. We might not have to kidnap her after all."

"You don't think he would hurt her do you?"

"Depends on whether he knows the difference between a bird and a human. But, he was hurting her just then right?"

"Right. Scary."

Later, when I got home, Nana was busy in the kitchen preparing dinner for the family.

"Hey Nana. Why is Mom asleep on the sofa?"

"We had an incident at the gym this morning."

"Is she alright?"

"Oh dear, she'll be fine. The sugar goblins from all that soda she drinks started fighting back right in the middle of our workout."

"I see."

"She ate a few donuts to help her recover, so she'll be okay dear."

The whole way home, I couldn't get Pam off my mind. All this time I thought she was living in a perfect world. Though I thought those things, I knew that life was never perfect for anyone.

"Nana, have you ever known anyone in a boyfriend girlfriend situation or a married couple for that matter where the guy is angry, aggressive, and maybe even abusive?"

"Can't say that I have dear, but most times, those situations aren't so clearly obvious to outsiders." Nana lifted up a rolling pin and an orange and placed the orange on a cutting board. "I will tell you that whoever puts up with it is in a sad situation." Nana paused then violently slammed the rolling pin downward, smashing the orange. "Because I wouldn't. Why dear? Is there a situation that needs correcting?"

"No. No. Just wondering really."

With a wide smile on her face, Nana raised the rolling pin up in the air once more. "As long as that's all it is, but if there is ever a problem, let me know. I got connections. I can mobilize a senior citizen lynch mob at the snap of a finger. We'll get gangsta."

I chuckled. "I'll let you know."

"They should teach about those types of issues in the school system. Probably more important than remembering the name of some fellow who rode a horse through town screaming that the British are coming."

"I couldn't agree more. Hey, I meant to ask you. Are you going out with that guy again?"

"He didn't get any strikes with my three strike policy, so I don't see why not."

"You met his driver?"

"His grandson, Devin?"

"That's the one."

"Polite young fellow."

Greer and Nathan crossed the kitchen heading in the direction of the pantry. "Hey Nana. Any snacks we should worry about Miranda?"

I replied, "Why? You got the munchies?"

Greer pitched Nathan a package. Neither of them answered my question, and they left the kitchen quickly just as Nana smashed the rolling pin back down on the orange.

"I'm cooking dinner here!" She paused. "Boys."

I added, "With a very small b."

The phone chimed; Nana continued cooking as I accepted the call.

"Hello?" I listened. "Oh, hi. How did you get my number?" I waited. "Oh, yeah I wasn't thinking."

Nana cleared away the smashed orange while watching me speak on the phone.

"Are you sure?" I turned away from Nana. "Okay. Saturday. Bye."

I must've looked shocked. I'm sure I look shocked. I mean, I was shocked.

"What is it dear?"

Almost in complete denial, I hesitated.

"Miranda?"

"Date."

"What?"

"Date. Saturday."

“Oh. Can I ask who?”

Suddenly I wasn’t able to speak sentences. I couldn’t believe it. A date. I’d never been on a date before. Even though I was allowed at sixteen, someone had to ask me first. I thought the event was something that would take place years from that point—maybe even in college.

****

Viewing Greer’s computer screen, a picture of Miranda covered with whip cream centered Nathan’s Facebook wall.

“I thought you wanted to lay off Miranda?”

“It doesn’t matter; she isn’t going to help us with Pam. The years of living under the same roof with you has taken its toll. We got to think of a better plan.”

“Your best battle plan is the one that involves a quick retreat,” Greer recommended.

****

Still reeling from the argument with her boyfriend earlier, Pam pecked at her dinner plate.

“Pam is something bothering you? You’ve hardly touched your food,” Pam’s mother inquired.

“If I eat, you disapprove, and if I don’t, you disapprove.”

“Darling, please don’t behave like a local. I hope this improper attitude doesn’t come out when you’re with Trent.”

“Attitude with Trent. Funny.”

“I’m just suggesting that a refined young man might not take well to such a tone from a young lady.”

“You’re absolutely right Mother. It’s me. I’m superficial. I flirt. I eat. I don’t eat.”

“Medication darling, medication.”

“Medication Mother, medication.”

EIGHT

Because Christian retained jaded feelings about people in relationships, I was unsure of what his response might be about the news. Surely, he understood the day would turn up that I'd date someone. Maybe he didn't. Maybe he believed that we would be attached the hip for the duration of our lives. We never discussed such matters, I suppose. Not that I needed to justify, but it was just a date; it was not like I'm getting a promise ring, wedding ring, or anything of the sort.

As much as I had the urge to phone my best friend after the invitation from Devin, I decided to wait until the next afternoon on the way to rehearsal to share with Christian.

In what was the quietest ride in the muscle car ever where the engine even took on a new tone. I hoped he would share what he was mulling over inside before I spent the next two hours monitoring Pam's onstage movements.

"Are you going to say anything?"

"Not sure I know what to say. For the first time in my young life I don't have an easy slogan to roll off my tongue."

"For me, can you just think of something clever to say? Anything?"

"When you get hurt, I've got two shoulders?"

"Something positive? Less jaded."

"Let my mind work this one out."

Christian became withdrawn and distant. Something changed. I could honestly say that I'd never seen Christian so vulnerable. So hurt. Appearing so lost. I felt completely horrible, and though I'd done nothing wrong, I sensed I had betrayed him. Like, I'd just confessed that I was cheating on an intimate, longtime companion.

Christian slowed the red car near the front of the school.

"Hey, I think I'm going to run and get some coffee."

Though it wasn't out of norm for him to leave and come back, something in his tone solidified that he was less than approving of my planned outing with Devin.

What was odder, Christian wasn't a coffee drinker. OCD, ADD, and caffeine are like oil, water, and air.

"Okay."

In the course of the whole conversation, Christian's eyes peered straight forward through the front window, focusing on something clearly invisible to me. "Okay, so I'll be back."

The moment proved even more surreal when the fire engine red sports car left the curb at a snail's pace. No smoke. No markings. No high-pitched squeals. Like a very slow exhale on four wheels.

As I was on the sidewalk heading to the auditorium, I continuously glanced back over my shoulder. Oddly, Christian had stopped, sitting motionless. Motionless at first with both hands resting on the steering wheel, then Christian's arms went stiff, then relaxed, and it appeared as though he was taking deep breaths and exhaling. His mannerisms revealed volumes about his feelings, but the entire range of those emotions, I had no way of knowing. Was he coming back? Did he find the words he wanted to say?

Just when I was expecting those actions, as Christian would do, the car peeled forwards with urgency while smoke plumed as the car darted side to side while picking up speed. Was that an angry jolt from the launch pad? It was hard to differentiate.

****

If there were a pop quiz about the afternoon rehearsal, I would've failed miserably. My thoughts were scattered, and I disconnected entirely from almost everything happening in the room. There was stuff going on: people shifting props, others moving from one side of the stage to the other, and that's all I mentally noted. If the whole world had lost its head, I was onboard the crazy train.

I resurfaced from my alternate universe at the conclusion of two-hour rehearsal. My biological timekeeper detected the end of the session from the tone of Mr. Stancil's voice, much the same as the eyes detect the sun setting causing the body to create hormones that causes one to fall asleep.

"Good Pam. Now, I have to remind you to work on your expressions during those key words that will assist in delivering the believability of your character's connection to them."

Mr. Stancil had better watch himself; apparently, he had no idea what she was capable of doing. He would never know that, invisible to the human eye, she had swooped in and mangled his jugular vein as he fondled his keys near the front door of his home.

****

The sign posted on the brick column clearly forbid skateboarding on the sidewalk, including the porch area. Nathan and Greer ignored the warning since there was time to waste before Pam's expected departure.

Greer hopped his skateboard up each step. "Have you come up with something brilliant to say to her, cream puff?"

Nathan spun around, skidding to a stop. "You really don't know anything about girls do you?"

"Since you're the expert, I'm putting it all on your plate."

Nathan's foot tapped the rear of the board, and he clenched the two front wheels with his hand. "Girls don't want to hear a rehearsed conversation. They want it to be natural."

"Excellent plan Romeo. It's sure to go as well as the last time."

"I got this." Nathan preened, spinning the bib of his hat to the side.

"No doubt."

As usual, Nathan's armed flicked upward catching Greer, causing Greer to lose balance on the four wheels and stumble. Pam was in the vicinity.

"Easy," Greer suggested.

When Pam neared, Nathan asked the first thing that popped in his mind. "Is Miranda coming out?"

Stunned at the question, Greer's mouth hinged open.

"She should be right behind me." Pam flicked her long hair behind her shoulders.

"Thanks." Nathan nervously grinned, his shy eyes darting.

When Pam moved out of earshot, Greer rolled slowly by Nathan and whispered, "Smooth. Real smooth. Peanut butter smooth."

"What?"

"You sandwich! I can't decide if I should write this moment down in my book of important things to remember or not. Is Miranda coming out? That was all you had to say?"

"I had to break the ice."

Greer placed a cupped hand to his ear. "Do you hear that?"

"Hear what?"

Smiling Greer said, "The sound of ice shattering all over the Northern Hemisphere."

Nathan clutched a butt cheek. "Choke on a cheek, chump."

****

Pam closed in on her parked car where Trent paced back and forth, the monster snarling.

"Trent, I told you that I wanted to cool it for a while."

"Yeah, it looked like you were cooling it while you were talking to those two turd knockers just a second ago."

"This is so worn out."

He fumed, "You're so worn out."

"Whatever!"

"Whatever?" Trent copied in a female tone.

****

I caught on to Nathan and Greer rather quickly. One single post on the public Facebook wall gave it all away. Nathan mentioned that he was in love with a singer and it wasn't me because he knew better—he knew I would slug him in the kisser. I put the pieces of the puzzle together, which explained why they were constantly hanging around after school hours—and conveniently close to where Pam would be. We weren't having an afternoon brownie bake off, after all. After Nathan posted that humiliating picture of me doused in whipped cream and tagged my brother in the photo, I monitored their postings more clearly. And there it was—a hormonally enraged quest for love confessed in a public arena.

Christian hadn't returned from getting coffee, and after his departure and seeing it was two hours later, I was not sure if he planned on returning, so I asked Devin to give me a lift in the event that Christian never showed.

I wasn't the least surprised to find Nathan and Greer hovering nearby. "You two look completely guilty as hell."

"Of what?" Greer questioned.

"I don't know. Uh, stalking."

If they were stoned or stupid, which I always suspected, they might not get the hint that I knew what they were up to. It was worth a good chuckle, Nathan getting the girl. Pam? Ha! She might dropkick the quarterback for a stoned, skinny skater? Ha! Nathan didn't even have enough money to buy her lubricated meat at the mall, so how exactly would that work, the date? Might he take her to one of the free skate parks? No doubt, he had had one too many dates with the chief already.

Seemed that the school parking lot was destined go down in history as the place where confrontations go down. When Devin and I surfaced, the players waited in position for the battle. Without any whistles blowing, the action happened all at once as though we were watching a movie play out right in front of our eyes.

Trent propelled Pam against her car, and about the same time, Christian's loud car roared across the marked spaces rapidly skidding to a stop, which produced a high pitch squeal and dark smoke. The driver side of the muscle builder bolted open, and Christian soared out of his seat, the engine still purring.

"Hey touchdown! She's not a football! Take your effing hands of her before I attempt a field goal with you fat leather head!"

Releasing Pam, he rotated his position. "You? Field goal? Hardly!"

Christian charged closer. "Right. With the size and shape of that melon head, it would wobble off to the right."

Trent grunted. "Look, we don't need your help here! Just get back in your shiny car, brush your hair, and carry on!"

Christian thrust two hands out at his sides. "I didn't ask if I was invited to the party! I crashed."

Trent inched nearer to Christian. "You know, it might be worth it to see if I could take you. Who knows?"

Christian's chin rose outward, and his brow lifted. "Who knows? At least I'm not a bird or built like a girl."

Was this really happening? I panicked as the jock and Christian stepped even closer, close enough for fist to reach the other's face. I was sure they could smell each other's breath. Becoming part of the script, Devin intervened in the action.

"Whoa guys."

Nathan and Greer lurked behind me speaking gibberish. "James Dean has stepped into the lion's den."

Greer thumped Nathan's ear. "Come up for air or come down out of the clouds. Pick one."

Nathan was just as confused as I was. "Dude! English! Speak English!

I detested fighting, but when Devin swooped in, I found him to be even hotter than before. Why was that? A genetically passed down mechanism geared to mate with someone with strength and the ability to protect their partner maybe?

There was nothing cordial in Christian's thoughts about Devin's intervention.

"New boy, you better step aside. My buddy here is about to learn a new meaning for the word sacked!"

Both Christian and Trent pressed forward, which caused my anxiety to heighten.

"Christian!"

Personality number three practically foamed at the mouth, "I'm ready for this. I'm ready for this one!"

"Good! The next time you hear the letters QB, it will stand for quail brain."

Devin had wedged himself in between Christian and Trent, though that was not enough to slow them down as they inched closer. I was expecting a balled fist to take aim at a target, and then someone would throw a punch; then to my amazement, with one try, Devin shoved both of the growling attack dogs backwards.

Greer mumbled behind me. "Somebody has been drinking milk."

"How do you know that?" Confused, Nathan questioned.

The distance Devin placed between the two of them presented the two with a moment to count to ten and take a deep breath. While hovering behind Trent, Pam was just as hysterical as I was, but whatever was going on between those two caused this situation, and I couldn't believe it when she reached out and tugged on Trent's sleeve.

"Trent, let's go," Pam said.

Christian was just as surprised. "You're leaving with him?"

Christian heaved forward in the direction of the loving couple, though Devin quickly reached out, snatching Christian's shirt holding him with a firm grip.

"Let it go," Devin suggested.

I added, "Christian, please? Let it go."

By then, Pam and Trent were withdrawing to Pam's car. Full force, Christian yanked away from Devin, leaving a slight tear in his shirt. "Man, get your hands off me! Who are you anyway?" Breaking my heart, Christian faced me as he smoothed the sides of his head. "Are you even serious? Him?"

There wasn't even time for a blink before Christian turned away and abruptly entered his car. This launch confirmed his anger when the tires squealed for minutes, leaving a long, black mark across the spaces marked with white lines. Not breathing, I choked on the smell of burning rubber and my dear friend's scathing words.

Nathan rambled to Greer, "Your sister's sister is going to need new tires real soon."

Stunned, Devin said, "Wow."

"Right. I've never seen Christian so mad. Ever. His eyes. Something was different in his eyes."

"Anger will do that."

Greer chimed in, "Is all the excitement over?"

"Whatever that was about? Miranda, so, yeah, uh I think this means your driver isn't coming back. You still need a ride?" Devin grinned.

I had a sudden need to be kind. Either that, or I'm high from chasing the dragon-smoke from melting rubber anyway.

"Sure." I motioned to Nathan and Greer. "Do you two need a lift too?"

"Does he drive like that maniac?" Greer wanted to know.

We made it home safe, despite Greer's concerns. Devin's car was newer, quiet, and there were automatic windows. I didn't have to work out to fasten my seatbelt. All those thoughts made me sad, though. I missed the rumble. What had just happened?

Nervously, I rambled, "Hey, thanks for the intervention. That could've gotten completely out of control. Worse than it was, I mean. Thanks for the lift too."

"No worries. Saturday then?"

"Saturday."

I left the car, Greer followed, and Nathan was last pulling himself from the backseat.

Waving, Nathan said, "Thanks for the ride James."

Greer and I walked just ahead of Nathan.

"Greer, why does that twizzler keep calling him James?"

"Draft Miranda. A draft. A large draft."

"Greer, my young prankster brother, that is a gale-force wind."

****

"I didn't mean that. Why did I say that?"

Though it was hours later, Christian spoke to himself—or maybe to the car he loved. He'd driven around endlessly, with no clear destination. His sanctuary lived within the metal panels and frame that made up the red car.

Reaching the top of the familiar hill, Christian shut off the headlights. Slowly, the car proceeded in front of Miranda's house, passing. After circling the cul-de-sac, the car picked up speed and retreated from the neighborhood.

Sitting on the bed reading, Miranda believed she was hearing things. Getting up, Miranda moved to look out of the window of the two-story mansion where she concluded it wasn't the memorable rhythm of an old engine humming on all eight cylinders after all.

After the battlefield cleared, the couple spent the rest of the evening together. Trent didn't make it home by the time he had quoted his mother earlier that day. If anyone present for the war was watching Trent and Pam as they parted company, they wouldn't believe the scene—a lengthy goodbye hug, the kiss, but this is how codependent people behave. Personality number one was doing his job.

****

Trent dealt with his father's drinking for most of his life. At times, the drinking was heavier than others, but nevertheless, they were all difficult. The moments his father stayed on the wagon accumulated on one hand. Those periods were livable, but Trent and Karen both knew that inside, the alcoholic's craving was napping with an unquenchable thirst. For two years now, the alcohol consumption had increased—and so did the violence. Karen received the verbal fire, and her son often assumed the role of a punching bag. Nothing was ever good enough for the alcoholic, and everyone else was to blame for his money problems and his headaches.

Each victim in that family existed at a breaking point, and the person responsible was far from reaching his rock bottom.

Trent's father sat fueled and waiting. Karen waited as well, but fueled with the force of the negative effects of adrenaline. Late, Trent emerged in the foyer.

"You can't be trusted! Not one bit!"

Afterwards came crashing, grunts, and the vibration of bodies slamming into the walls. Hidden in a different room, Karen covered her ears, closed her eyes, and sank to the floor. Her words, her screams, built, rising a level each time.

"Stop it… STOP it… STOP it! STOP IT!"

Nine

Early Saturday morning, Nana cornered me in the kitchen insisting that I let her treat me to a day of shopping and a trip to the salon. She radiated more excitement about my first date than myself. Well, I lie, but as my Nana often mentioned, my parents were overly humbled, and I surmised it was rubbing off.

My parent suddenly decided that sixteen was far too young to go out on a date, but abiding by their own rules, they weren't going to stop me. Although, I did have to sit through the lecture that I assume most girls sat through, but as I said before, I knew it was important to keep quiet during a parents' talk. Why parents acted so nervous during these conversations is another question for the list. Their eyes shuffled around, and their speech emitted mostly in Morse code, kind of. We learned the mechanics in school, and I thought they should just cut to the chase and say, "Please don't have sex until we're dead" or "Teenage boys are possessed with evil spirits that they have no control over. They will lie, cheat, steal, and beg to get what they want." I know what they want, and it doesn't begin with the letter L. Girls want the letter L, but boys seek anything they can get, even if it's only second base. Love was something they felt for their mothers.

We were finished shopping, and I rested in the salon chair listening as Nana explained in detail what she wished for my new look. She brought pictures too, to help visualize the pending miracle. I would've settled for a different conditioner scent. I'm a simple girl.

"I don't think we're going to need the forklift. A little clip here and a little wax there. What about this one?" Nana modeled one of the pictures she ripped from a magazine.

"Hot! Cayenne pepper hot girl," the hairdresser expressed, approving of the look.

"It will cause my daughter..." Nana coughed. "My older sister to have a major hot flash."

"You stop." The hairdresser was laughing.

Well, Nana gave a secret away. Now, I knew why my mother had been so grumpy lately. It wasn't merely the sugar goblins fighting back, inertia; Mother Nature had joined the party.

By the end of the day, I had gone through a mini makeover. Once I dressed and twirled around my room, I believed I heard applause from the google-eyed group lounging in the white wicker chair. The makeup part even looked okay even though I wasn't a big fan of the stuff.

Thankfully, for me the hairdresser worked her magic because I wouldn't know where to begin. Base, foundation, eyeliner, lip liner, and so on. All the steps I mean, it's similar to painting a Picasso with a-paint by numbers kit on a blank canvas. While going through the makeover, I suggested we keep the layers to minimum because I at least wanted to look like myself. Keep it simple. I'd bet that all over the world there are men waking up next to women and not knowing who in the hell they are. How could they after forty layers of crud rubbed off on the sheets in the late hours of the night?

Checking myself out in the mirror of my dressing table, I noticed the pendant—the pendant Christian and I had traded in a vow of friendship. I hadn't stopped thinking about Christian—what happened in the lot, but I had to get it out of my head and keep focusing on what was about to happen in my life, my first date.

It's really silly all the hype about a first date. I was more amazed by the fact that Devin, a hot guy, had asked me out. There had to be something wrong with his vision. What if he showed up in my living room wearing glasses and changed his mind? Buddha, Buddha, Buddha. Red string. Mary, Joseph, Jesus are you here?

I was relieved that my immature brother and his airhead friend had already gone trolling the mall for the evening. Those two not being present saved me from enduring a moment of torturous teasing and an opportunity for a Facebook addict to snatch a photo, embarrassing me further by putting it on display for the world.

I never expected anything less from Nana, so when I revealed the total look from what we had achieved earlier, she was pleased with the outcome. My mother, not so much—I think she was sweating, having a hot flash maybe.

"Dear, all I have to say is you better not stand to close to any chocolate bars."

My mother refrained from making many comments. I sensed straight away that Mom was nervous about the date because while the three of us were talking, she gulped soda out of a can like a man drinking beer during a rowdy football game.

****

Saturday nights, the mall was habitually crawling with citizens from the surrounding communities. The chain specializing in easily swallowed hamburgers held the typical line that extended across the aisle, almost reaching the table closest to where Pam and Trent found themselves eating.

"I think my mom is about to leave him." Almost vacant, he peered across Pam's head.

"What would you do?"

"I couldn't leave you." Splitting near the middle of the burrito, the contents oozed out from the tear, dropping onto Trent's shirt as he clamped onto a hardy bite. "Crap."

"That stain will come out if you get it quick."

Trent scooted away from the two-top table. "Be right back."

Spying had consumed most of their free time, but Nathan and Greer had no idea that they would see Pam when they set out for the mall. Nathan left the game store with Greer behind him when he noticed Pam across the bridge that led to the food court where she was eating. Spotting her, Nathan halted in his tracks, and not paying attention, Greer bumped into him from behind.

"Dude, wtf? You can't just stop walking without getting out of the way."

Nathan fixated and didn't respond.

"There is another store down at the other end of the mall. I can't believe this one doesn't have that game."

Nathan still didn't react.

"Yo, what are you looking at?"

"Pam."

"Oh no. The rest of the night, you're going to be a zombie. We won't even need Zombie III."

"Okay, okay. Just remain calm," Nathan said to himself.

"Nathan? Are you talking to the voices in your head? I mean, I'm calm."

"Okay. Take a deep breath," Nathan said.

Greer clenched Nathan by the arm. "Dude, snap out of it. Let's go."

"Where are we going?"

"We are going to talk to Pam. This is ridiculous," Greer said.

"Going to talk to Pam?" Nathan's voice cracked.

"That's what I said."

Greer tugged at Nathan's arm, leading him like a puppy attached to a leash. “It’s obvious that her boyfriend is a tool, so make a move. You’ve been following this chick around acting like a virgin since the beginning of the school year.”

“I’m not a virgin,” Nathan said defensively.

“Yes you are. I’m a virgin, you’re a virgin, and Pam is, well, Pam is probably not a virgin.”

“You’re a virgin?” Nathan asked.

“Yes, stop acting so macho. Besides, if you keep this up, you’re going to be searching for a way out of Cherry Land when you’re thirty.”

“Why would I be in Cherry Land? I’m not leaving the state.”

“Forget it. You’re never getting any,” Greer replied.

“Any what?”

“Really?”

“English dude. Speak English. The older you get the crazier you talk,” Nathan said.

“Well, the older you get, the dumber you get.”

Nathan and Greer crossed the bridge and entered the area designated as the food court where Pam still sat alone.

Greer approached. “Hey Pam. What are you doing here?”

****

My nerves calmed slightly just about when...well, I lie, they probably rattled for the entire night. I thought Devin looked handsome before, but that was nothing compared to his appearance when I met him in the living room. That look was definitely put together with an agenda.

The restaurant he chose was very impressive, decorated in the exact palate as his voice, red velvet. Devin behaved so kind and did all the appropriate things I imagined a guy would do on a date. It didn’t seem rehearsed, though since Devin carried himself with a genuine politeness.

From magazines and shows, I gathered that girls were supposed to limit food intake on a date, yet I scoffed at that idea. The glossy shine of the icing on the desserts alone was an invite to dig in. My face wasn't pretending to be something it wasn't and neither was my appetite. Fact or fiction, I agreed with the statement whether Marie Antoinette said it or not. Let them eat cake!

"That is unreal!" I lifted my fork and savored another bite.

"Good, right?"

"Why can't things like this be healthy?"

Devin grinned. "Moderation and sit ups."

"Nana says skip the moderation, but she is all for the workout."

"Thanks again for coming."

"Thank you for inviting me. It's my first time you know? I didn't know what to expect, honestly."

"Really? Well, I hope it has been fun so far."

"Well, I mean, I have fun with Christian, but this is a different kind of fun." Oh no. Did I mess up by mentioning another guy? Whoops.

"Ah. So if you don't mind me asking, what's his story, your story, the two of you?"

"We've been best friends since kindergarten. My brother jokes around and calls Christian my sister. It's funny and not so funny at the same time."

"Yeah, I guess most guys wouldn't be fond of being called a girl. Kind of ego crushing in a way. So, why do you think you two never made the leap? You know from being friends to a couple?"

"My grandmother asks me that all the time. To be honest, I've wondered briefly, but it passed. We've never discussed it really."

"Is he gay?"

"I haven't asked. He hasn't told. I wouldn't care."

"I wouldn't care one way or the other either. I just asked because, I mean, look at you."

"As of now, I only know, just like everybody on the planet, he has issues."

"Don't we all though? I sensed that in the parking lot, yet he seemed caring. Now, that other guy, I don't even know him, but there was an overwhelming energy of rage."

"Interesting. Yeah, Christian's parents had a turbulent existence. Christian was never treated badly, but I gather that witnessing two people who allegedly love each other rip each other apart did a lot of damage to a little kid who was trapped in the middle as the referee. And Trent, I don't know what to say about him. He scares me."

"You have to wonder about love. Love can bring about so much pain, yet love can bring about so much healing."

"So you'll agree that therapy should be mandatory for everyone?"

Devin laughed. "Without question."

****

Pam spoke to them, but she just wanted Nathan and Greer to go away. Not that the boys repulsed her, but Pam remained aware that their presences presented the potentiality for the rest of night to transform into a living hell.

The conversation lasted longer than the usual passing exchanges between an auditorium and a school parking lot. Enough so, Pam grew insurmountably uncomfortable, but it was too late. Just before the young hopeful fool and his sidekick departed, Trent exited the men's room, continuing to dab the stain with a wet napkin. When he looked up, number three curled deep within, his arms stretching overhead, both eyes flicking open. Fully alert, the monster clinched the football player from the inside. The intensity of coming to life caused Trent's skin to glow, as the tiny red lines shot across the whites of his eyes.

****

Gravel crunched underneath the weight of the skateboard pressing downward on the pavement. Nathan twirled the board around pausing just short of Greer's position. Proudly, Nathan's foot tapped the wood; the board ascended vertically balancing on its tail, and with one finger resting on the tip, the skateboard spun in circle.

Flat handed, Greer lightly smacked his confident friend on the back. "You did it. You actually did. You talked to her!"

"See, I got this! Ryan Sheckler can't compete with this. I got game."

"And there he goes folks, right back into the gale-force winds."

Nathan preened, and Greer let him have his moment.

TEN

We decided after the Deadly Sinful Decadence, that's what the desert was called, to go for a walk and skip the confines of a movie theatre. Devin mentioned that he thought movies were not good for first dates since they lasted nearly two hours, and that time was better suited for getting to know each other. He was full of surprises.

"I can't believe it's less than a month away," Devin said.

"Aren't you nervous about getting up there in front of all those people? I'd be a wreck. I'm nervous for you."

"Don't be. I'm not."

"Pam's not."

"She might be; you never know." Devin paused. "You know, you have a uniqueness when you sing that sounds better than her."

"Whatever."

"Believe what you want."

"Thanks for that, but she has the right packaging to sell the product."

"Silly. I'll say it again. Look at you."

"Really, I'm not fishing for compliments. I'm just realistic. I have a mirror. I kind of feel sorry for her."

"Yeah? Why is that?"

"I used to watch her from afar. I thought everything was perfect. I don't know, but I get this feeling of emptiness from her. Like she has been forced to fill her cup with a drink she doesn't like."

"I get that."

"Sad really. I know how that story plays out. Christian and I call it a belt made out of ice cream and sadness."

Devin smirked. "A belt made out of ice cream and sadness?"

"Yeah, you know. Forty, indentions in the sofa and a muffin top."

"Hilarious."

"Sorry, I keep mentioning his name. I guess that's wrong of me."

"Miranda, don't worry. I'm not one of those jealous guys. Though I know nothing about him, he must be interesting if you've been friends with him for so long. I believe that if things are meant to be, they will be. If the two you are destined to be together, then I am centered enough that I could and would be happy for you."

****

The plastic tray crashed to the floor just after Trent's slamming fist caught the corner as he pounded the table. Vibrations popped a filled paper cup upward causing the ice and soda to splash across the two-top. The surrounding diners thought it was an accident, but Pam knew the truth; he was angry about what he saw as he was coming out of the bathroom.

Pam didn't speak; she wouldn't dare. She didn't even care that her bland colored skirt was soaked and clearly see-through. No doubt Trent noticed, accusing her of enjoying the fact that everyone in suburbia could see her girly panties. Then again, the monster growled saying it didn't matter because most of them had already seen them since she was the local whore. Pushing further, he suggested that she wrap herself with his jacket because he didn't need any further embarrassment.

Trent growled, "Get your shit, and let's go."

Her boyfriend cupped Pam's elbow in the palm of his hand, guiding her through the crowded mall. It was merely a couple of minutes to get to the exit, yet Pam felt that the walk of shame seized hours of time. Remaining silent, Pam sniffed back the tears. She'd cried enough. She'd had enough. She realized that it would never change. The personality she thought would go away if she loved him enough seemed not to care one way or the other.

With Trent driving, Pam's car zipped passed Greer and Nathan who were skating near the mall entrance. The horn blared breaking their dedicated concentration to mastering tricks.

"Rude."

Nathan recognized the car. "See, she was saying goodbye."

"Breathe, Nathan. Slow deep breaths."

"It's cool. I got this."

Vile continued spilling from monster's mouth, spewing accusations both new and foreign to Pam.

With Miranda spending Saturday night elsewhere, Christian was resigned to spending his evening with someone he loved, his car. Pulling out of the car wash, where Christian had just replenished a glossy layer on the tires of his date, he recognized the car passing just ahead. Acknowledging to himself that there were two people inside, Christian made a right and trailed Pam's car down the dark two-lane road.

Trent's break from raging was only momentary. The second the lights of a car hit the rearview mirror, he recalled that he had heard the distinctive roar before. Further glancing, looking left into the side mirror, he identified the fire engine red classic and acknowledged that it was following intentionally close.

"Well, look. The hero is back to save the day. What, are these boys just following you around? The tramp, like a dog in heat?"

By now, after holding them back as long as she could, tears traveled Pam's face with streams of mascara. Along with the tears, until now, she'd held back speaking since leaving the food court.

"Let me out of this car!"

Christian firmly gripped the wheel, each bump in the street felt in the steering vibration. With his foot, Christian inched the accelerator closer to the floorboard. The rumble under the hood rose a level. "Now my chance has come to truly do mankind a favor. This time it will be so worth it. Call me a hero."

Trent followed suit, speeding up as Pam pleaded desperately.

"Let me out of this car!"

"Shut the hell up!"

Pam was ready to give up. Not only give up trying to please someone, but give up in the fight—even if that meant risking her life to get away from the monster, Pam reached for the door handle. "I mean it Trent. Let me out of this car!"

"Silly tramp."

Pam lost it, and her screams tinged around the car.

Through the rear window of the car just ahead, Christian watched the action in front him as Trent's arm swung to the right slamming into the side of Pam's face.

Inside Pam's car, Pam tugged at the door level. "Let me out of this car you son of a bitch!"

"Shut your mouth!"

Staying tuned in to Trent's car, Christian saw Trent swerve from one side of the road to the other; Christian knew he couldn't leave them alone. On the passenger side of Pam's car, the door cracked open.

****

I'm sure that most girls experience the same feelings after a pleasing night with a cute boy. We don't want the night to ever be over. Couldn't it stay like this forever?

While out walking, Devin had placed his arm around my shoulders.

At first, I thought about boys, their minds, and their endless pursuit to get more than pleasant conversation. For a moment, I speculated that Devin's gesture was the point in the night where I found out that Devin had an agenda. Turned out, as far as I knew, he didn't. Good for him though, I would've hated to have kick in his teabag or break one of his fingers.

Against my wishes, date night was concluding, and curfew loomed as we made our way to my average, middleclass neighborhood. That was when I heard sirens, and before long, the lights flashing in hues of blue appeared behind Devin and me.

Devin eased the car to the shoulder. "Uh oh. What did I do?"

As the police car sped by, the draft shifted Devin's car up and down.

"Guess you're in the clear."

Within seconds, sirens wailed, lights blinded, and another police car zoomed by going even faster.

"Whoever they're after did something serious." Devin reached for the shifter.

Next, two ambulances approached quickly with the full spectrum of red and white warning lights accompanying the screaming distress signals.

I turned, watching them out of the rear window. "Wow, good thing we're getting along, well, I assume. We might be here awhile."

Devin beamed. "We are."

I should love the fact that Devin affirmed that we were getting along, but suddenly I felt very uneasy—like, I forgot something. It was a sense of panic, or it felt like all the sugar in my body had vanished. Had the goblins from the Deadfully Sinful Decadence begun fighting back?

"I just got this horrible feeling," I told Devin.

"Those lights and sirens will get your heart racing for sure."

"Yeah, I guess that's it." Was that it? I reached for my neck. Was I wearing a necklace? Did I lose it?

****

I'd seen how it all goes down in romance movies. I had read about it in books, and now, I wondered exactly how to handle the end of the night. As Devin and I lingered just outside of my house, I hadn't noticed my silence.

"You got quiet. Are you okay? Still shaken by the sirens?"

"Is this a normal feeling at the end of date?"

When I got in inside, I found Nana and my mother waiting in the kitchen. Mom probably sat at the kitchen table wringing her hands the whole time I was out. I suspect she had to confirm for herself as to whether or not my face revealed the glow of becoming a woman.

I'm not quite ready to take that leap. What kind of girl does she think I am? Oh, that's right: the speech where she explains that she was a teenager once too. That explains what went on back in The Go Go's heyday, confirming my belief that she had once let her hair down and let words with sound come out of her mouth.

"Hey dear." Nana was first to welcome me home.

"Hey."

"So, how did it go?" Nana asked.

"Not that I have anything to compare it to, but it was fun."

"Did you give him a wet kiss?" Nana asked.

Mom seized her chest. "Mother!"

"Sister. Well, was it hot?"

"Mother!"

"Not any detail to tell. He was a perfect gentleman," I replied.

"Oh, thank God," Mom expressed.

"Mom, did you think that I would…"

"Miranda, I worry. You'll understand when you have kids of your own. I knew you would do the right thing. The intention of others worries me, though. I was a teenager once too you know."

"Mom, relax. There was nothing wet, and nothing touched. We talked about people and their demons. That's all. Talk."

"Sound like a deep conversation for a first date," Nana concluded.

Joining us in the kitchen, my younger brother, who always held a silly demeanor, looked as though he were three-years-old and lost his puppy. It wasn't a stoner look either.

"What's wrong with you?" I asked.

"I'm so sorry. I'm so sorry."

"What is it?" I asked.

Worried, Nana and my mother rose from the table.

Greer peered downward towards the floor, "Miranda…"

ELEVEN

As the passenger side door opened further, Trent's foot quickly pressed the brake pedal, and the brake lights on the rear of Pam's car illuminated a bright red.

Since he was following too closely, Christian had no choice but to slam on the brakes himself. The speeding muscle car tilted forward as the brakes grabbed hold of the speeding tires. Inside, with both hands fighting the manual steering wheel, Christian struggled to turn the left.

Tires skidded across the loosened gravel on the blacktop while the rear of the car twisted to right. The screeching continued, and once the right front tire left the pavement, the car hit the soggy marsh on the side of the road. There was nothing Christian could've done.

Due to the force of the plunge downward off the road, the heavy weight of the vehicle lifted one side of the car from the ground. Speed kept it in motion as the car spun upside down, while the entire rear section of the car rose in the air as if the car were twirling on a small section of the front bumper.

Though it was mere seconds, it seemed to be an act playing out in slow motion. As the beloved car violently crashed to the ground, Christian's bloody contorted body, twirling, flew from a ripped section as metal crunched together causing sparks. Along with the thunderous thud, windows shattered, and the fragments of glass dotted the grass. The noise was so prominent it stifled the final grunt as Christian's torn body thumped, hitting the ground.

Several minutes passed before the emergency services arrived. It didn't matter. Christian was dead.

****

"…there's been an accident."

When Greer nervously spoke those words, somehow I knew. It wasn't one of those 'It was bound to happen feelings.' It was more like I knew that a piece of me was missing. That piece was my best friend, someone I'd swear I had known for many lifetimes, if there were such a thing.

"Christian is…"

His name was all I needed to hear before I blacked out. Greer didn't need to say that Christian was dead. His face answered that, and I could tell by the way he said "Miranda," and the way he said "accident." Greer wasn't about to tell me that someone had simply broken an arm.

****

Days later, I had to take in details about the accident in small doses. Those specifics were so hard to hear, and the sadness was overwhelming. It was killing me, but I wandered over and over and over how long Christian had to feel pain caused by the brutal force of the crash. Naturally, every time I thought about it, I burst into tears.

Christian's parents relayed to us that the emergency workers suggested that most likely, Christian died on impact, but I pondered how they could be so certain. Was there scientific evidence to back up their theory? Furthermore, at what point during the hellish event was impact? When the car left the roadway? When the metal sections of the muscle car separated? Or when Christian's beautiful bloodied body dropped from the night sky?

Christian's mom greeted us near the entrance of the funeral home, and after the formalities, she let us know that the casket would remain closed. That's when I lost it. The wreck was so bad, they couldn't show his body? On the other hand, was the damage so severe that we might not recognize his face? His pretty face.

Once I snatched hold of the pallbearer bars on the casket, I refused to let go, and my fingers turned bone white while my mother and father attempted prying them free. I fought hard, holding on tightly until Nana and Devin hovered at both sides, calmly coaching me. True, Christian wasn't here, but there was nothing rational when it came to grieving. At least I'm not one of those people who actually attempted to climb inside the coffin.

Funerals are horrible. Of course, anger is part of the grieving process, and as I listened to the eulogist speaking in front of the chapel, I fumed. These people knew nothing about Christian. Under the circumstances, they probably thought it was insensitive to mention the car, but Christian loved that car. Once they mentioned he had been a good student in school. Christian? Not once did they make mention of how Christian looked out for the well-being of others, the many times that he rushed in to help some nerd that was getting the crap beat out them by some overzealous high school jerk. His hair, how could they miss that? Even at school, he was referred to as that guy with the hair, and instantly, anyone knew to whom they referenced.

Devin was very sweet throughout the whole day of the services. Thoughtfully, he helped me out the car at the cemetery and guided me across the lawn to the burial site. As they lowered the casket into the ground, Devin held me up as I weakened and leaned into his firm body.

My parents tried to get me to leave with them, but I wanted to stay and watch the workers shovel the dirt back in rectangular hole, as morbid as it sounds. Devin remained at my side when my family decided they'd prefer not to watch, though they weren't openly admitting those thoughts. But I knew. I got it.

****

Back across the lawn, the family waited by the car. Nana patted tissue underneath her teary eyes. "This breaks my heart. It's so hard to see her go through this."

Greer added, "I knew the way he drove wouldn't turn out so well."

Nana placed her arm on Greer's shoulder. "It's sad, but I'm thankful she wasn't in the car with him."

Greer remained serious. "His driving is only part of the story though."

Nana caught the inflection in Greer's voice that suggested there was more going on behind the scenes in her grandchildren's lives than she knew. Christian's too and she loved him just as much, though his life was over.

****

Once the workers completed their task, I inched closer to the mound of dirt where I dropped a rose from my hand as more tears welled in my eyes.

"Miranda."

A vaguely recognizable voice spoke my name. I turned, looking around, but only Devin waited nearby, and it wasn't his voice that I had heard.

"Miranda?"

I veered around once more as I slowly backed away from the plot where I joined Devin. The cadaver of my best friend was hidden away, and all that remained was Christian's voice in my head.

Devin and I covered the grassy grounds, meeting up with my family at the top of the knoll. We all hugged—even Greer and I. embraced. Once we exchanged niceties, my kin loaded into their car, and I stepped inside Devin's car. Devin was so handsome in grief-wear, might I say, but when was he not?

Devin broke the silence of the mournful ride. "I'm floored that no one is in trouble and being held accountable for what happened."

"The way it happened—I mean, I knew he was reckless, but that was so by chance. So random," I said.

Devin lowered the radio volume. "Not to take away from your feelings, your loss, but maybe it wasn't so random. Everything has reason, happens for a reason, I mean. With our simple way of thinking, it's hard to understand these situations. Who knows what was going on that night, why Christian was following them. Whatever we don't know, despite the tragedy, some higher good was served."

The familiar voice in my head, comforting, spoke out. "He is right."

I pivoted, glancing at the rear seat, and then I turned back facing the front of vehicle. "I'm sure you're right. If I could think straight, I might see that. I can't stop hearing his voice. It's killing me."

Again, in my head, Christian spoke, "You've forgotten the pact."

Once again, I glanced.

Devin softly reached for my hand. "It's tough losing someone. That's why I think it is important for people to use their words cautiously. Life is unpredictable, and words can haunt forever."

"That's true." The voice agreed.

I veered around again. "I can't believe Pam jumped out of that car."

"Trent's story," Christian's voice stated.

"That's Trent's story," Devin suggested just as fast.

"That's what Chri…" I stopped myself.

"What?" Devin questioned.

Surprised, Christian asked, "Wait, you can hear me can't you?"

"Nothing," I said to Devin. "I don't know what I was going to say. I'm losing it."

"Miranda?" The voice pleaded.

Devin squeezed my hand. "I'm here for you, always."

Christian agreed. "Through math, through art—even through death, we won't part."

****

For two days, Nathan was lost without Greer. Just like Christian and Miranda, the two were very seldom apart. Since kindergarten, through first grade, and on to Boy Scouts, Greer and Nathan were buds.

Clicking the mouse, Nathan's Facebook wall popped on the screen.

"Take it off," Greer scowled.

"Dude, why? It's hilarious," Nathan said.

"Now is not the time," Greer growled.

Nathan's mood was typical, but he hadn't spent two days with a grieving sister and friends and family at a heartbreaking funeral. Though Nathan was an airhead, he got it on some level. With a few clicks, the picture of Miranda plastered with whipping cream vanished.

"Sorry bud," Nathan said.

"It's okay bud, just not right now."

Greer and Nathan bumped knuckles.

****

Would I get over this?

After my grandfather's passing, I was similarly distraught, and as time passed, the pain eased. It took Nana a little longer, but eventually she gathered herself together. There were moments throughout the years though, that her emotions crept in, mainly on holidays and anniversaries. Nana's room was down to one framed photo of the man she spent over half her life with, and I guessed that was enough for her. Losing Christian was no different, right? I would get over this wouldn't I?

Sitting at my dressing table in the dark with only a streetlight shining in through my window to the world, I stared into the mirror. Is there meaning to everything as Devin suggested? Is there any need for searching deeper to define the purpose of this specific event? Could

Mary, Joseph, and Jesus help ease the pain tearing at my heart? Might the Buddha have the answers?

How could I continue? He was my rock, the encourager, the one who I unconditionally loved—the one who helped me see things from a different prospective, the lighter side of a dark world. And all the while, he kept his own troubles buried deep within, behind a pretty face.

"Oh Christian."

Faintly he whispered, "Don't be scared."

Gazing into the mirror, I gasped. "I'm going mental."

In the mirror, a quick flash of light reflected from behind me, causing a quick inhale.

"Miranda."

Gasping, I swiveled around, scanning the room. Then I returned to the mirror, closing my eyes. "Oh God. Oh God. Oh God."

"Please," he said tenderly.

"Oh God."

"Please don't be in fear, or I must go."

I eased around slowly, opening my eyes and catching another quick flash of reflecting light. Shirtless, sitting on my bed, his back erect, with legs crossed, and his hands placed gently on his lap, Christian smiled. I saw something recognizable adorning his neck, the other half of that silver friendship pendant that rested on the table behind me. His pendant had caught the light seeping in the window.

"I wish I could show you how I look."

I thought, surely, I'm hallucinating as I stood up, leaned backwards, resting against the dressing table.

"Wh… what do you mean? I… I think I see you."

Christian chuckled. "Look, you're not crazy. Take a deep breath. You see me as you remember me in my Earthly body. In heaven, you will still recognize me, but I'm a young child. In fact, everyone who is already there is young. But not young in an Earthy sense of the word."

"Ar… are you a ghost?"

Again, Christian laughed. "We'll just say, in spirit."

"This dream is so real."

"Miranda, you're not dreaming. I served my purpose."

"So what Devin said…"

"Yes, though I can't reveal the specifics."

"What are you doing…"

A knock at my bedroom door halted the conclusion of my question as I shifted to face the door. "Yes?"

Swinging open the structure, Greer padded through the doorway flipping on the light switch, and just like that, Christian was gone.

"Were you on the phone?"

"Oh, uh, no."

"Nana wants you to come down for ice cream."

"O..okay. I…I'll be right down."

When Greer left the room, I called to him. "Christian?"

CHING. To the right of me at the foot of the dressing table, my half of the friendship pendant had fallen to the worn carpet.

****

Greer slid up to the bar top, lifting a spoon.

"She is up there talking to herself. She'll be right down."

Life already resembled normality in the kitchen. If anyone felt the same as I did, trapped in a tunnel, it was not blatantly obvious. But I was slipping fast into a world of reflective lights and apparitions. Would I notice a difference in anyone's behavior anyway?

Sitting next to Greer, Nana positioned a whopper of a treat in front of me. "Sweetheart, I made you a cure-all banana split."

"Hope it can cure crazy, since she was up there talking to herself." Greer shoveled a spoonful of ice cream in his mouth.

"I wasn't talking to myself," I responded defensively, while taking dainty bite of my treat.

"You said you weren't on the phone, so who were you talking to?"

"A ghost."

"See Nana, complete wack job."

Removing more cherries from a jar, Nana spooned them on top of my surprise. "Well, Greer, we're all wack jobs in one way or another. When you were little, you swore that a pint-sized old man sat on you bedpost and talked to you until you fell asleep. I always wondered why you never put up a fuss about going to bed like most kids." Nana spoke the truth.

"I did not."

"Yes you did. You just don't remember. You said it was Grandpa."

"Ah, you're making that up to make twisted sister feel better."

Well, no doubt, Greer was his former self. A couple of hours with Nathan, and my brother was as good a new.

"Ugggh."

That's what Greer said the second I plopped a large scoop of banana split on the side of his face.

"Cool down turd," I told Greer. "You got me on trouble once because you swore to Mom that I closed the little old man up in the microwave."

"I did not."

"You did. I got grounded for teasing you. Mom said, 'Stop telling your brother you trying to kill the little old man.'"

"Well, he was sitting on the corner of that plate. You put grandpa in the microwave."

"See, busted."

Nana's treat didn't soothe my emotional state, but watching Greer squirm as the freezing cold ice cream slid down his face brought about some semblance of normality.

I wondered about the little green man. Had he been sitting on that plate of pancakes I placed in the microwave? Was it Grandpa? Nathan didn't even know him, but he sure pitched a hysterical fit. Though I was only heating my breakfast, my mother, convinced I was teasing, gave me a good talking to about scaring my brother. Suddenly, I had an epiphany. That explained what was wrong him. Greer was damaged goods from a short lifetime filled with pranks and talking to old little men.

Twelve

Luck granted Pam favor on the night of the accident because she hadn't been injured severely. Evidence of severe bruises covered her body. Her leg was broken, but the black eye and the gash in the center of it was a result of Trent's rocketing fist.

Unless it involved shoes, clothing, or decorative pieces for the home, Pam's mother was hardly the doting type. Smoothing the protective cream on Pam's injury had nothing to do with helping Pam. No her mother's motives were more in line with maintaining the image she worked so hard to maintain since her college graduation and wedding to a financial well-to-do. Girls with battered faces didn't frequent the country club scene. In that regards, there were far too many questions, which needed politically correct answers to avoid the gossip amongst the socially elite.

"Oh dear, I hope you're not left with some dreadful blemish that will haunt you for the rest of your life. What were you thinking?"

Even though the words gave it away, having lived with a superficial parent for over a decade, Pam wasn't fooled by the nurturing gesture. "It wasn't my fault," Pam replied.

"Of course it wasn't dear."

After the accident, Pam never bothered telling her family the specific details of what led to tumbling from her car. At the scene, she let Trent do all the talking. Mainly, because she was in shock, couldn't speak, and there was a dead person nearby. The night was tragic enough, and Pam detested playing twenty questions—questions that she was sure would lead to someone twisting the truth and making it out as if she had put herself in the situation because she chose the wrong dress or wore too much eyeliner. Going further, her mother may have asked if her behavior was inappropriate for such a well-mannered young man, one that was hard to come by in such a small town?

Since the day Pam arrived at school with a backpack that garnered so much attention, Pam's mother handpicked and approved the children that were best suited for her daughter. It didn't matter if Pam liked anyone or not. More important scenarios should be taken into consideration. What neighborhood did they live in? Where did their parents work? What model car did they drive? Were their parent married or divorced? From a genetic standpoint, were they decedents of a serial killer or anyone with a mental illness? The process of elimination left Pam to choose friends from a very short list.

From an early age, Pam's mother coached her to believe that a majority of society was inferior if they could not live up to certain expectations. Over time, it became a subconscious effort on Pam's part—that is, until she began to rebel. Once Pam could see through the façade, she began to question herself, her family, and the status quo.

The damage from the early training needed much undoing. The reasons for making certain choices in life were not so obvious at first. Such as picking a boyfriend who had three different personalities, where each of those personas fed a need for Pam. Abuse was not a choice, but Pam felt deserving of that treatment because her mother always made Pam feel as though her behavior caused someone to react in such a way.

"Darling, you must make better choices. I hope they can find someone to replace you."

"Mother, there is no dancing for my part. It's just singing. Mr. Stancil said there would be no problem reworking the intro."

"You can't be serious. Show your face in public like this? I don't think that's the best decision. You just can't."

"Do you think anyone will care if I have a black eye?"

"For the rest of your life, that's all anyone will remember. Who can enjoy the singing if they're distracted by this horrid mark on your face?"

****

Though supportive, Devin was unsure if it was the best idea to accompany me to the impound yard. Thinking about it for several days, I decided that I had to see it. True it would be painful, but I just had to.

Since the funeral was a closed service, I needed something, anything, to put this tragedy in tangible terms. The spot where the crash happened couldn't bring conclusion or whatever it was I was searching for. There were markings on the pavement, glass pebbles on the grass, and the shoulder of the road itself looked as though someone had scratched the surface with a tractor of some sort. I swear I saw random splatters of dried blood, which caused me to vomit, and that made it oh so real.

Devin suggested that bloodstains aren't what I saw because it was common for the Department of Transportation to clean up oil, gas, and body fluids by using cola. What the eff? And people drink that stuff? The producers of those products must be in cahoots with the lubricated meat marketers.

In what I considered to be totally morbid, Christian's parents, or possibly a relative, had staked a wreath nearby. Why would anyone want their memory secured at the location of their hostile demise? It seemed cruel, and besides, I know for fact that spirits don't linger around their place of transition. No, they hang around in bedrooms, sitting on beds, or in kitchens sitting on the edge of dinnerware terrorizing little boys. Unless, Greer was correct in his calculations that I was indeed a wack job, I'd witnessed one of them, a spirit.

Devin agreed to go with me, and the lot attendant was kind enough to guide us through the winding trail of twisted and broken down cars. There were all kinds. No vehicle was excluded in the grand game of highway bumper cars. Here, it was unimportant where Christian's car was parked.

The attendant's phone rang, "J&J. One second." The attendant paused, lowered his phone, and pointed toward a path in front of us. "You kids stay on this row. You'll run right into it. I'll catch up with you in just a minute." He lifted the mobile to his ear, "I'm on the way. Tell them to put in lot B."

With a crusher compacting cars two rows over, Devin and I continued on the trail between the stacks of metal waiting to be recycled.

"I know I asked already, but are you sure you want to see this?" Devin asked.

"I know. I'm morbid, but since the casket…well, I just need to see it."

The fire engine red, I recognized immediately. Caused by contortion of the front end, the four-hundred and whatever numbered engine had heaved upward. To the right of that, a muddy tire with scant areas of shiny black showed through folded underneath the right quarter panel. There was nothing familiar about the protective top of the muscle car, which was severed from the lower cabin, except for one length of metal the size of a baseball bat that barely kept the roof attached.

"Oh my God."

Steadying myself, I neared the remnants, my stomach beginning to churn. *That* was real. It was difficult to get my head around it—this car, the love of my best friend's life, this killing machine.

Devin neared me, placing his reassuring hand on the small of back. Peering across the metal through what resembled a window opening, I trembled at the sight of the driver's seat that leaned to one side, half of it torn away from where the bolts were welded in the floorboard. A brilliant quick flash of light blinded me, if only for a second. Gasping, I leaned in closer.

"Woah, you kids don't get to close. That ripped metal can be razor-sharp. Might cut something slap off."

A quiet and tender voice called to me. "It's okay. Take it."

Noticeably, I inhaled, and in one rapid motion, hoping the attendant wouldn't notice, I scooped up the pendant from the seat of the car. Adhering to the kind man's suggestion, I backed away from the mangled man killer. As I did so, I noticed a torn piece of bloodstained fabric twisted in the seatbelt slide. Still backing up, I counted my steps. One. Two. Three. Then, slipping away, everything was black.

Something was wedged underneath my neck when I came to, and Devin was dabbing my forehead with cool water. "Miranda?"

Opening my eyes, over Devin's shoulder, Christian grinned as if he was enjoying the sight of me sprawled on the ground.

Devin dabbed. "Miranda?"

"You've got to stop doing this Miranda," Christian said as he smoothed the hair on both sides of his head.

"What happened?" I asked, confused.

"You passed out. Are you okay?" Devin replied.

"Yes. I'm fine."

"Blood still gets you doesn't it?" Christian questioned.

"Yes it does," I answered Christian.

"What?" Devin wondered.

"Stop thinking about it. I know you are. You're doing it right now," Christian said.

"I'm trying not to," I told Christian.

Confused, Devin patted me. "Maybe you should drink some water."

"Didn't Yoda say there is no try only do?" Christian asked as he gathered the strands of hair that rested between his brows.

"Like now is great time for the teachings of Yoda," I said.

Devin turned his head to face the attendant. "Think we should get an EMT?"

"Yoda has some great advice. As a matter of fact, Star Wars has some great advice. I always liked those movies," Christian said.

"Yoda was creepy looking," I told Christian.

"Miranda can you hear me? I think you should try to drink some water," Devin said insistently.

Christian swooped down to a squat. "Why do you think every time someone passes out or gets stressed out or sick that people think they need water?"

"Here drink some water." Devin twisted the cap.

"Because they're trying to drown you so that you'll shut up," I suggested.

"Ah, never thought of it that way." Christian smiled.

"Miranda, I'm not trying drown you," Devin said.

I lifted myself to my elbows. Christian stood as Devin slid his arm to brace me from behind. With his free hand, Devin positioned a bottle of water up to my lips. "Here, just one sip."

"Tell him you'd rather have orange juice." Christian laughed.

"I hate orange juice," I said.

"It's water," Devin replied.

"No, not that," I told Devin.

"Better yet, tell him you want pickle juice," Christian said.

"Why would I want pickle juice?" I asked Christian.

Looking worried, Devin addressed me seriously. "Okay, we need to get you to a doctor."

Christian burst out laughing.

"Stop laughing. This is not funny," I said.

"Miranda, I know it's not funny," Devin said in an even more concerned voice.

"No, Devin. Not you," I tried to explain.

"What do you want me to do? I'm just trying to help," Devin said.

"Tell him it would help if he got you a donut and some pickle juice," Christian declared, with a laugh.

"Donut?" I asked.

Devin turned to the attendant. "She has hit her head. Call 911."

"He is panicking," Christian bellowed. "This is hilarious. I bet the next words out of his mouth are…" Christian snapped his finger.

Christian and Devin spoke at the same time. "Everything is going to be okay. Just relax."

"I guess you're a mind reader up there?" I asked.

They spoke in unison again. "Breathe. Take a deep breath."

"Yeah, that's the other thing they tell people too," Christian said. "Breathe. Just breathe." Christian slapped his hand together.

"What do you want me to do?" Devin panicked.

"Tell him to call 911 and have them bring you a donut and pickle juice," Christian kidded.

"That's funny," I replied.

"What's funny?" Devin worried more.

"He is going to pee in his pants," Christian yelled.

"You foresaw *that*?" I yelled back.

"Foresaw what?" Devin motioned his head to the attendant, suggesting he phone 911.

In a more serious tone, Christian suggested, "You don't need 911. You need to get off the ground."

"Miranda?" Devin asked.

"Stop. Everybody stop. There are too many people talking at the same time," I screamed.

"Okay. Sorry Miranda. But one more thing before I find something else to do. He is thinking you're crazy right now," Christian state, matter-of-factly.

That was it. Christian burst out laughing, and by the time I blinked my eyes, he was gone. I pondered the pickles. Oh God, Devin was going to think I was whack, wasn't he? Minutes passed before Devin spoke again.

"911 will be here in just a second. Here, take another sip of this water, and then take a long slow, deep breath."

I burst out laughing. People did say that! God, I missed Christian so much. Well, in an Earthly sense I meant.

If any moment of life should've ever been captured on film, it would have been that moment. When Devin explained the event to the emergency medical technicians, I rolled with laughter at every word. He said Yoda, and I laughed. He said pickle, and I laughed. He said drown, and I smacked my leg laughing so hard I was unable to catch my breath. In smothered English, I said, "I need oxygen." The big EMT in the blue jumpsuit gave Devin all his attention then responded in a serious monotone voice, "She must have hit her head pretty hard."

Once the drama was over and Devin was taking me home in the car, I cracked a couple of times. When something is funny, it's funny. What was I supposed to do? During the ride, Devin's face looked like he'd sucked on a pickle, yet he too surged a few chuckles, basically, laughing at me laughing. Several times, I assured him I was okay. How could I explain it really? Oh, Devin, sorry about that. I was trying to listen to you and talk to a ghost at the same time. And thinking about saying that made me laugh.

Back at my house, I left the room while Devin explained what happened to Nana and my parents. I couldn't. I just couldn't. My stomach ached from laughing so hard already.

Greer sneaked around the corner, joining them in the living room.

"I've been trying to tell you guys this forever. There is something wrong with her all right, but I don't think it's because she hit her head. I've got a suggestion. What do you guys think about having Miranda institutionalized?" Greer asked.

Nana normally kept out of parenting affairs, but she stood up from the sofa, pointing to the second floor. "Tadpole, go to your room."

"What did I do?" Greer waived his palms in front.

Nana squinted, "W-a-s-a-b-i!"

"That was you?" Greer questioned as he retreated backwards.

Nana crept a step towards Nathan. "Does that goofy friend of yours, Nathan, does he know about the old little man that sits on your bedpost?"

Greer stuttered, "Mom, Nana's scaring me."

What a baby! I blurted another laugh in the kitchen where I was spying on the conversation.

Still backing from the living room, Greer pointed to the kitchen. "See, see, see?"

Nana inched closer. "There is this picture of you when you were four-years-old peeing in the snow. I wonder, just wonder if your best bud would post it on the Facebook?"

"MOM!"

That little twerp had some nerve trying to get me committed. I meant to remind myself to swipe the nudie shot. I would've passed it out in the school lunchroom.

Despite all the loony moments, Devin was charming. Even his worried expression added pleasurable elements to his adorable face. He was a keeper. Maybe my mother should've worried because I desperately wanted to kiss him as he left later. And, I wanted to grab his bubble butt, just to see if it was real, of course. I'd heard about that padded underwear for men. Just checking, that's all, to make sure he wasn't part of Pam's neighborhood, where synthetics reigned.

"Sorry about today. Thanks for the water," I told Devin.

"You scared me to death."

We hugged, my hand resting on his belt loop. I almost did it. That butt was calling. I pulled back. "I guess I will see you at school tomorrow."

Devin reached for one of my hands. "You will. Can I call you later?"

"Sure. You know you can."

"Okay, so I guess around nine. I'll call you after I shower and settle in bed for the night."

I wanted to say, "Pick me, pick me." But instead, I said, "Okay. Thanks for today."

Devin fetched his key from a back pocket. "My pleasure."

I was so jealous of that damn hand right then. That hand must love its life, always by Devin's side. Always within reach of any part of that firm body, that butt, and his… Stop. I must stop. My mother would have a heart attack, and it wouldn't be because she was struggling to get through the grocery store.

THIRTEEN

If there was any way to make Mondays less Monday, I'd be all for making those changes. On a positive note, I would get to see Devin at school, and that almost made showing up worthwhile. His butt would be there, too.

There were questions—lots of questions about Christian and the accident. Devin served well as a bodyguard, fending off the gossipers. I didn't even know half of the students that hovered around my locker, a quarter of the others, I hadn't spoken to since that memorable backpack episode, and the rest lost my interest the second they addressed me by saying "hey shawty." Christian was suddenly a celebrity for something other than his infamous hair.

****

Rehearsal commenced right after school, and since the performance dates were getting closer, Mr. Stancil required everyone involved in the production to participate every afternoon up until the debut of the musical. He was more nervous than usual, verging on hysterical, more so than the cast. Mr. Stancil continuously reminded us that *Whole World Lost Its Head* was his baby. And he was joining the world in the head loss.

Pam no-showed for rehearsal, which surprised me because I had seen her earlier in the day at school. She was hobbling on crutches, and though Pam was quite a stretch from where I stood, her face didn't seem all that bad.

Panicking, Mr. Stancil's hands shook ferociously as he pressed in my direction with urgency. "Miranda, Miranda, thank the show tune gods you are here. We have a situation." He paused. "Oh, let me back up. I apologize for sounding so rushed and uncaring, but if I blow this production, the school will stop funding these events if it doesn't draw in a large crowd. So, what was I going to say? Oh, yes." His pace slowed. "Miranda, I'm so so sorry about Christian. Such a tragedy. You look well, but you must be devastated."

"Thank you Mr. Stancil. I appreciate that, but if it is okay with you, I'd rather not discuss it too much, well, you know…"

Mr. Stancil reached out and took my hand with a sympathetic squeeze.

"Yes. Well, that settles it then. I'm not really allowed to say things like this, but what the heck. I'll pray for you."

"Thank you for that."

"Now, where was I? Yes, Miranda we have a situation."

"What's wrong?"

"Well, Pam…" he paused, his eyes shifted to the flooring. "Since Pam, you know…" he glared up. "Pam is not going to make the performance. I need you."

"What?" I heard what he said, yet it wasn't registering.

"Miranda, you're the understudy. You have to take her place."

"Oh."

"This is my baby; please, gods of theatre, say that you can pull through for me? I need you. My head is simply hanging by one thin thread."

"Oh."

"Please tell me you're okay enough to do this."

"You can do this. Tell him you can do this." Christian appeared next to me.

"Oh."

Mr. Stancil squeezed my hand. "I'm desperate."

Christian slid around me, pausing at Mr. Stancil's side. His face curled, making a cute sad face. "Please Miranda," Christian begged.

"Mr. Stancil, I…"

Christian's face returned to normal. "Mr. Stancil nothing. You can do this, Miranda."

"Would it help Miranda, if I told you this was Pam's idea?" Mr. Stancil asked.

"It was?"

"It was," he confirmed. "She spoke with me during lunch today."

"Well, I…"

Distracting me, Christian hopped up onto one of the theatre seats, and began dancing, his arms flinging around in the air. I think he was singing Y.M.C.A. quietly to himself, his arms spelling out the letters.

"Well, what?" Mr. Stancil prodded.

"I…"

Christian jumped from the chair. I say jump, but I think he sort of floated downward. Floated is not the word really. Something more along the lines of a graceful slow motion. That is what spirits do right?

"I nothing. Miranda, unless you want to hear dogs barking every night for the rest of your Earthly life, you look that desperate, middle-aged man straight in his queer eye, smile, and tell him that it will be the greatest honor in your young life—that is, unless you enjoy lying there at three o'clock in the morning listening to the never-ending howl of every mutt within four blocks of your house. They can hear me too you know. I will sing to them—steel bending, might I remind you. My voice is not heavenly."

That's when I discovered that sprits never breathe. How on Earth, though he wasn't Earthly, could someone say so many words in a row without taking a breath? I needed a sip of water after his rant, and I hadn't even spoken a word.

Mr. Stancil, with sweat beading on his brow, glanced at his silver wristwatch.

"Ruff." Christian slumped on all fours. "Ruff, ruff, ruff."

Accidentally, I shouted, "OKAY! OKAY!"

Mr. Stancil's upper body jerked back, not expecting such an exuberant reply. "Well, I guess that settles it. I'm pleased that you're so enthusiastic about it."

Standing up, Christian smoothed the sides of his head, and his second motion gathered the strands of hair that rested on his forehead. Next, he pantomimed YMCA once more.

Swirling around, reviving his panic, Mr. Stancil scurried down the aisle smacking two hands together. "Time is ticking people. Let's go, let's go, let's go! Props in place! Lighting, warm up the motherboard." Mr. Stancil continued clapping until he stepped three stairs up and stopped onstage. "DEVIN!"

Following his ghastly summons, Mr. Stancil flicked all ten fingers at stage left, stage right, center stage, orchestra, lighting, and the audience area. Was he sprinkling fairy dust or glitter? I watched as he kissed the ten appendages. Then, making fists, he praised the gods that he'd referred to earlier.

"DEVIN," Mr. Stancil shouted again.

"Yes, Mr. Stancil. Over here."

Hearing Devin's red velvet voice, I glanced across the mostly empty rows of theatre seating. Smiling, Devin's shoulder lowered as he parted his way through a group of girls that surrounded him like a fan club. Devin scampered down the aisle, getting closer to Mr. Stancil, forgoing the stairs; he hopped up on the stage. It wasn't my imagination at work; the huddled group of teenagers giggled while watching Devin's every move.

Thinking he would reappear, I whispered, "Christian, are you watching the beginnings of the catfight?"

Christian didn't answer; I guess he had found something else to do. How did that work exactly, the showing up randomly? Is there a magic word, a specific topic of conversation, and poof, the dearly departed joins the action? What else was there for Christian to do anyway? Does he linger in a misty undertow waiting for someone to rub the genie bottle?

If his spirit were around, I was sure he would declare, "I told you so." Then Christian would continue with his theories and quote book chapters. Now, that his prediction had manifested right in front of me, I speculated where that left me, but I knew, it placed me exactly where Christian suggested, needing a shoulder to lean on.

Lost in a world of thoughts, I hadn't noticed Pam hobbling into the auditorium. Like Christian, instantly she materialized at my side.

"Hey Miranda," Pam said softly.

Snapping out of a daze, I responded, "Oh, hi."

"I guess you were blindsided by Mr. Stancil?"

"I had no idea. I thought you were still doing the show."

"I mean look at me. There's no way."

"Considering what happened, you look okay."

"I am, well, kind of. Still, I just can't."

"Thanks for…," I stalled, "Thanks."

"I…I'm sorry about Christ…"

I interrupted. "Don't say anything. Thank you, but it's hard."

"Right. Same here."

Cutting Pam off, Mr. Stancil broke out shouting for anyone involved in the production get started with whatever was his or her assigned task. Lastly, causing my heart to race, he bellowed my name, summoning me to the stage.

"MIRANDA!" He snapped his fingers and pointed, indicating where I should end up.

Pam reached out, touching my arm lightly. "Good luck."

"Thanks."

Surprising myself, I remained calm throughout the practice session. If any nervousness surfaced at all, it had nothing to do with my reservations about singing for a crowd. Anyone watching in the seating looked stuffed and goggley-eyed, so it wasn't much different from the worn carpet in front of my dressing table back home.

For the entire two hours, I couldn't help but notice the girls watching Devin—the same as I had done on the first day of rehearsal. At the right moment, one of them held up a flirty wave and smiled, giving me the desire to snap each one of her boney little fingers, but I pondered if the effort to do so was really worth it. Determined not to be a part of the catfight, I made a decision.

****

Four days since seeing Pam felt like an eternity for Nathan. Greer would have forgotten all about her had it not been for the accident and the fact that her name kept coming up in conversations as his family discussed the tragedy.

Nathan sped up his pace through the corridor, but Greer lagged behind since every few feet, a fellow student stopped him to inquire about his sister's best friend.

"Dude, would you hurry up!" Nathan yelled over his shoulder.

"Chillax hound dog. People won't mind their own business."

"Right. They're even asking me stuff. I do what I do, just play stupid."

"Play stupid, Nathan?" Greer jabbed.

Not getting it, Nathan replied, "Yeah, act like you don't know what they're talking about. It works."

"Guess so. I never know what you're talking about," Greer said.

"Don't be such a turd."

"So, turdface, I guess you still think Pam with a black eye is the hottest thing since the iPhone?" Greer asked.

"Are you kidding me? Crutches and Band-Aids? Hot! Really hot! She and I could play doctor," Nathan replied.

"Oh God, I think I'm going to vomit."

"Dude. What did you have for lunch? Maybe you should drink some water and take a deep breath."

"Nathan, really?"

"What?" Nathan asked.

While Nathan and Greer continued their pursuit of Pam, Nana and Miranda's mother were back in the gym.

Four days of accumulating stress and sugar from the soda bled the life out of Miranda's mother. Huffing and puffing, she clamped onto the rails of the treadmill while sweat drenched her hair. In perfect step, Nana worked vigorously to up her pace on the incline.

After the timer buzzed, Nana had to help Miranda's mother who was struggling to get down from the machine. Her daughter was too worn to move on, but Nana was just warming up.

"Come on girl." Open handed, Nana smacked Miranda's mother on one side of her rear end. "You've got to fit that oversized red caboose in a dinner dress!"

"MOTHER!"

****

When it was over, Mr. Stancil had survived several mini heart attacks. Never had I seen him so worked up, but lucky for me, his frustration mounted over silly things, mainly lighting and prop placement.

Quite relieved at how I handled the vocals on the song that begins

'Freeway fell into the bay,' Mr. Stancil whipped his hands together and bragged. He would never know I'd performed the song before in front a group of stuffed friends sitting in a wicker chair. Impressing him even more was how closely I'd come to mimicking the lettuce-chopping dance without hurting someone onstage—or lobbing someone's head off, for real.

Before exiting the bathroom, I phoned home requesting that my mother come pick me up, but dad said that she was sprawled out on the bed moaning and that he would be there in less than five minutes.

"Miranda, you did well!"

Feeling a little embarrassed since it was a first time Devin had seen me really let loose, I faintly smiled. Figuring I had no reason for keeping myself restrained, I let it all go, total abandonment. Remaining concerned about what others thought, well, I got over it. As people say, life is short, and if there isn't a tomorrow, it's even shorter in this moment. For some, that is a fact, so Nana was right. Avoid the potholes as best you can and eat the brownies, but do so in moderation.

Devin hoisted a backpack on his shoulder, "Are you ready to go?"

Uncomfortably, I answered, "My dad is picking me up."

Not able to hide the angst, I felt he could sense something was up. "Is something wrong?" Gallantly, he twisted his head to the side appearing concerned.

Of course, that's how he posed the question, with a slight tilt of the head. Most likely, chapter seven covered that—'Always seem concerned.' Christian wasn't around for reference, but I'm pretty sure it's noted in the 'How to get women Bible.'

"Devin, I just don't know about this."

"Riding home?" he asked.

"No. This. Us," I replied.

As I suspected, Devin eased down in a chair, a maneuver used to put an opponent at ease and make them feel superior. Textbook move.

"Has something happened? Did I do something?" he asked with even more concern in his voice.

"Look, I have to be honest. That's who I am. I don't want to get hurt. Christian had an opinion about guys like you, and when I saw all those girls hovering around you, I had to think about it."

"That's what you've been thinking about? Wait, guys like *me*?"

"Yeah. Handsome. Well dressed. Always gets a girl. I don't want to be *a* girl; I want to be *the* girl."

Devin flipped his palms up, resting his hands on his thighs, a sign of openness. "Miranda, I'm not like that."

"Maybe not. Let's just take it easy okay?"

"Miranda…"

An incoming text from dad informed me that he was outside, which rescued me from furthering the uneasy conversation.

"Listen, my dad's here. I'll talk to you later?"

"Miranda," he pleaded, but I left anyway.

FOURTEEN

Whatever the universe hid up its sleeves had me completely confused. Accepting what I thought was a hint, I went ahead and auditioned for the musical. An encounter with a handsome boy in a parking lot and then again in a driveway, I agreed to go on a date. Without warning, the divine order threw a curve ball. First the wreck and next the revelation that Christian was right all along about relationships. Perhaps these situations were meant to remind me not to be so critical about my humble place in the world—even if that place were in my room singing into a flatiron, appraising the world through a large window.

After taking a long deep breath, I decided I had to get back to my reality, mainly get back to being me—and to stop it with this fantasy.

"Dad, would you mind stopping by the grocery store? I need to pick something up."

"Sure dear."

At the store's entrance, I retrieved a shopping basket and headed straight to aisle number seven, the baking aisle. Removing all of the packages from the shelf, I positioned them in the basket. Nearly laughing as I caught him out of the corner of my eye, Christian, on the tips of his toes was perched on the end of some woman's metal shopping cart balancing with ease.

"How cool is this right? I got tricks."

Christian flipped backwards, somersaulting until he reached the far end of the aisle. I surveyed as he moved a few feet, taking a step upward, as though he were stepping onto a surfboard. That is exactly what it looked like too; he was surfing with no board and no water as he glided right in front of me with a big smile.

"Woo hoo!"

Closer to my end, Christian circled around the corner, and I hurried to see what he might do next. Reaching the end-cap, I peered in both directions. He was gone.

"Christian?"

Back home, I dumped my items onto the kitchen countertop and started stacking the small boxes so that I could put them away. One hand filled, balancing the stack, I headed for the pantry and opened the closure.

"BOO!" Christian shouted as the door cracked open.

Jumping, my boxes tumbled to the floor as I let out a scream.

"Gottcha!"

I bent over to gather the boxes.

"I'm baaaaack," he whaled in a poltergeist manner.

"You scared the hell of me."

"Sorry. I've always wanted to do that." Christian beamed with pride.

"Well, you *are* a ghost," I said.

"For lack of a better explanation." Christian joined me on the floor.

One after the other, I stacked the boxes again. One was a bit out of my reach. Christian inched near the box, and though he didn't touch it, his hand hovered just above the package. Then, like he was flicking a bug, the small box slide closer to where I was squatting.

"Well, did you see what happened today?" I asked him.

"I did. Congratulations, chickie."

"I feel bad for her you know?"

"Don't be. That night was real eye-opener."

"For her, but for you it was…"

Laughing, Christian added, "An eye closer."

"How can you take it so lightly? I mean, if I'm not crazy, I still see you, so it's not like you're gone, but you *are* gone. Well, you know what I mean."

"If you could see it Miranda. If the world could see it. Just for one second. If they did, tomorrow everyone would stop fighting. Weapons would be destroyed, the hungry would be fed, and those that feel unloved would know they are. And so much more."

"Did you…" I paused as tears fill my eyes. "Did you feel pain?"

"Don't get upset. I was out of that body before the first piece of metal impaled it."

"This might be a silly question because I don't have any experiences with, uh, ghosts, but will you always be here?"

"Not like this. Not visually. And I have to tell you, honestly that you will forget about this kind of talking to me, but you'll always have a feeling, which is the best I can do to describe it. Truths are for the other side."

"So, what are you doi…"

With her hands full, Nana strolled into the kitchen, ceasing my question about what he was doing here. "Hey dear. We had to catch up on the shopping," she said.

"Hey Nana."

Nana rested the bags on the counter, leaned in, and whispered. "If those two are a couple, not only would they have ugly babies, they'd be dumb as a bag of rocks. Those two boys drove me crazy. They kept talking, and I'll be damned how they understand each other because I never understood a word."

No skipping a beat, Nana and Christian expressed their thoughts at the same time.

"Can't wait to see what happens with the Jell-O," Christian said.

"What's with all the boxes of Jell-O?" Nana inquired.

When Greer and Nathan entered hauling numerous grocery bags, I realized that Christian was no longer there. Well, I don't know if he was or not.

"Nathan, if you don't stop stalking her, she is going to knock off your watermelon head."

"It looks like somebody already tried to knock yours off, flat face."

****

The rest of the week was a complete blur. By the conclusion of Tuesday's rehearsal, Mr. Stancil had lost a few more hairs from his balding head. There were a couple of incidents where he overreacted and ran out of the theatre swearing that he couldn't take it one more minute. I thought he was sneaking out for a drink myself because every time he came back he seemed mellower. Unless he was staying up late at night clamoring over the details of the performance, there had to be an explanation for his bloodshot eyes. He was a product from the sixties, though; he could've had a batch a brownies hidden in his office desk, for all I knew.

By Wednesday, the key elements of the show ran smoother than ever, and for once, Mr. Stancil finally relaxed. Sitting dead center of the row seating, he crossed his legs, clasped his hands together, pointed his index finger upwards, and rested the tips on his dimpled chin. If he hadn't smiled, I would've believed he was pretending the shoot himself.

Thursday made the third day that I kept my conversations with Devin limited to talking about the show. He tried; I'll give him that, but still, every effort that he made seemed like a page right out of the textbook. Though I tried refraining myself from observing, I noticed the girls still fawning all over Devin during the breaks. For that matter, a few of the boys were too, and that made me feel even worse about the situation because I knew the odds of winning a competition against those guys was impossible. Gay guys are always stylish, put together, and more forthcoming and blunt about what they're after. If Devin had an inkling of sitting on the fence with his sexuality, he would sway in the direction of boys since it was less complicated to relate to someone who had the same body parts. Honestly, if I couldn't be the winner in the feud, I'd rather him take the easy road. For me, that was less ego-crushing somehow.

The best part of Friday was not having classes, well, for the members of the production anyway. Since the first performance was later in the evening, my nerves had ramped up enough that I wanted to approach Mr. Stancil about sharing his stash of the chief. I wouldn't dare, however, because drugs aren't my thing, but it is funny to think about the shock on his face if I were to ask him to share his brownies.

For three hours in mayhem and madness, the production crew worked feverishly to put the final touches on the set. Mr. Stancil clapped, skipped, shouted, and sprinkled his glitter in the dark recesses of the auditorium. I was relieved to see Devin socializing with the boys more, which gave me one less thing to ponder before the show.

Once the glitter settled, we all parted for home to rest, relax, prepare, or panic.

****

Following the accident, police officers escorted Trent home that evening. Not that he was in trouble—the ride home was a courteous gesture on the part of the officers. Pam, in hysterics and injured, was carted to the hospital in an ambulance, leaving her car to be towed away by a wrecker. Since Trent was not the rightful owner, he wasn't allowed to take the car. Not that she would have, but Pam was in no state to grant permission.

Clever with his explanation of the event, he had won over the police officers. The fact that he was a football player aided in the appeal, of course, and when he suggested his father was a drinker, the officers volunteered to drop Trent off on their way back to the police station.

Even if he had asked the officer explain the hold up to his father, his drunken father wouldn't have listened or cared. All his father knew was that Trent had missed his curfew, and for the past three hours, Trent's father had listened to Karen worrying aloud about the whereabouts of her son. Making it worse, as she waited, Karen stared out the window and saw her son exiting the police car. Mentioning this to her husband only revved up his anger.

That night, with Karen screaming in the background, her only child and his father fought until they were bloodied, bruised, and exhausted. Furniture was out of place, lamps were broken, and sheetrock walls were caved in, but that didn't stop Trent's father from filling his glass with vodka, raising it, and offering a toast at the conclusion of the confrontation.

"I might be older, but I can still whip your ass," the drunkard said.

Karen did her best to help Trent with his injuries, but with the monster fully alive, he felt nothing—not even the four-inch gash above his eyebrow—not even the blood that filled his eye socket.

Trent pushed away his mother's hand. "Leave me alone."

The drunk slurred, "You hear the big baby. Leave him alone. Let him do whatever he wants to do. He does anyway."

Later, after the two had fallen asleep, Karen removed a suitcase from the closet, packed some clothing inside, and sat it by the front door. Her husband hadn't reached rock bottom, and if rock bottom wasn't beating one's own child, then she didn't know what it was—or if it would ever come. Karen's own child was no longer the little boy that needed protection for all those years. Karen knew she had failed her child, but it was too late to do anything to resolve that or even take it back. She couldn't step back in time, swoop the young boy up in her arms, and flee. It would get better, she had always told herself, but the proof was in front of her. And time was behind her.

Earlier, Karen had urged Trent to come with her, telling him that they would get help and start a new life, but Trent, or the personality that dominated him, refused, exclaiming that there was no way he was leaving his girlfriend behind. Still after all that had happened, he continued claiming Pam as his property.

Karen kissed the sleeping shell of her son, left his room, walked down the hall, picked up a suitcase, and exited. When the door closed, she knew that the next time she heard any news about her family, one of them would be in jail or dead. Did it matter really? Weren't they dead already? Weren't they prisoners already? She cried, realizing that inside, she was dying as well—from a broken heart. She cried because she knew she was freeing herself from a prison.

Lying in bed, not asleep, but with his eyes closed, a shattered son heard the door down the hall shut. Opening his eyes, the tears welled, and Trent wiped his cheek with a closed fist just before punching a hole in the wall next to the bed.

For hours into the night, he lay there fuming, seething, the monster feeding from the fuel. Not able to sleep, Trent eased out of bed and went to the living room.

True to form, his father's intoxicated body covered a portion of the rug in front of the displaced sofa. Trent inched closer, his feet crunching shattered ceramics, unafraid, his heart racing. Reaching for his fly, he eased down the zipper, removed his penis from the opening, aimed it at his father, and began peeing.

He growled, "Piss on you, you son of a bitch."

FIFTEEN

"Okay guys, I'm off. Wish me luck."

They didn't respond, didn't blink, didn't move, and didn't utter break a leg. Typical for that bunch, they clung shoulder-to-shoulder staring forward with no cares in the world. There was no sympathy, no advice, only watchful eyes. Concluding they were in shock because I had actually gone through with it, I retrieved my bag and left my stuffed googley-eyed friends to rest.

On the way out, I mumbled to myself, "Christian, where are you?"

I needed him then just as I needed him as the motivating force that led me to that moment. Is that why he came to me in the first place? I hoped he hadn't forgotten that I depended on him while he was off somewhere in space, time, whatever it is, and doing cartwheels creating an unexpected draft of wind to blow on an unknown victim.

Somewhat sure that I had regained control of the runaway train of a romance fantasy, I agreed to hitch a ride with Devin back to school. What an uneasy ride that was seeing as how I didn't know how to start a conversation, and I considered that Devin didn't either.

Still the gentleman, Devin opened doors, smiled his unforgettable smile, and used all the tools of the lady killer trade. I wasn't intentionally being cold, but my nerves were busy ticking in sync with every blink of the two dots that separated the minutes from the seconds on the digital clock on the dashboard.

Turning into the parking lot, the memories of Christian, his car, his attempt to save Pam from the Ham, and the upcoming performance weighed on me heavily. Not forgetting that, despite my decision to take myself out of the girl-group equation, on some level I adored Devin, but I couldn't let myself trust those feelings. Maybe he was indeed a vampire, and unknown to me, his magical appeal was still calling.

Inside, Mr. Stancil was relatively calm, but I supposed that at any minute, the dust would be flying. Oddly, Pam was backstage rocking back and forth on her crutches, which surprised me since I didn't anticipate her showing up for the event. If the roles were reversed, I would be far too humiliated to show my face, literally.

"Hey," Pam said to me.

"Hi. Wow, you look much better."

Pam grew emotional. "Thanks. Make-up helps. Thank you for doing this. I just wanted to come and wish you good luck."

I could tell that Pam was hurting. More was happening behind the exterior of the girl I thought lived on top of the world.

"My mother hates that I even enjoy singing. She'd prefer I make good grades, act like a stupid blond, and wait for a man with money to take care of me," Pam said.

"Pam, if you want to do this, do it. Trust me, I won't complain."

"No, I can't. I just need to lay low, get my head straight, and try to survive until I can go away to school. I'll be eighteen soon. Anyway, I don't want to put a damper on the night. I could talk about this stuff forever as long as someone is actually listening."

"You're sticking around right?" I asked.

"I don't think so."

"I'm sure that Mr. Stancil wouldn't mind if you hung out backstage. He is so nervous, he probably wouldn't even notice."

"Thanks for that. I only came to wish you luck, though. You know, you sing very pretty," Pam said.

"Thank you so much for that. I could so use Christian right now, his humor," I replied.

"Always here." It was distant, yet Christian's voice rang clear.

Pam halted, bobbling on her crutches. "He saved…"

Mr. Stancil burst through in a full throttle panic. "Ten minutes folks. Let's go, let's go, let's go!"

"Guess I better get ready. What were you going to say?" I asked.

"Nothing, you better hurry."

Pam limped down the corridor, heading in the direction of the theatre seating. The most popular girl in the school, and she doesn't have anyone to talk to? I thought that, but realizing the key point in her statement was the word listen. Hearing and listening are different verbs.

****

Beyond the school grounds, overhead, a dark cloud loomed as the weather person had predicted during the morning broadcast earlier that morning. Prepared, Nana brought along an umbrella, which she held in one hand, and the other gripped a bouquet of flowers that she picked up from the florist for Miranda.

Taking their spots in the theatre round, Nana was relieved when Nathan and Greer shared that they were parting to go to the bathroom. During the ride over, the two boys and their untranslatable conversation grated on her last nerve. Using the umbrella, she had already pecked one of them on the shoulder for farting in the backseat of the minivan.

Miranda's father agreed as Miranda's mother complained about the small theatre seating. Nana wanted to remark that the seats weren't the problem—that it was her daughter's caboose complicating the comfort. She kept it to herself though because the taunting at the gym earlier was enough for one day.

With the tips of his fingers barely touching the backrest of Nana's seat, Christian was in a full on handstand, with his face falling just to the side of Nana's head. His legs spread apart and then moved together resembling a pair of scissors in action. His face remained animated the whole time, making faces and lastly sticking out his tongue, like he was putting it in Nana's ear.

Faintly, his spirited voice suggested, "Take the flowers now."

Nana withdrew from the seating. "I'll be right back, I'm going to run to the back and give these to Miranda."

****

Nathan and Greer weren't heading to the bathroom as they said; instead, they were going to find Pam. As if that were a surprise. The second the minivan hit the quickly crowding school parking lot, Nathan had spotted Pam's car. Months had passed so his detective skills were more fine-tuned. He probably smelled her perfume from the ticket booth like a hound dog, and within the gibberish that Nana didn't understand, he and Greer trumped up plan to track her like a laser-guided heat seeking missile sailing through the auditorium.

When they entered the corridor leading backstage, Nathan held confident that fate rested on his side. Halfway, leaning against the wall, Pam stood sobbing into her hands.

Even though the hormones held the leash of Nathan's drive, his approach was deeply sincere. "Pam, what's wrong?"

****

Mr. Stancil made another nervous pass updating the countdown to his long awaited masterpiece. In my head, I repeated, Christian, Christian, Christian, trying to figure out the magic sequence that makes the genie poof to the surface. I concluded that I should've asked that question while he was present, along with asking him what he was doing here and who controls the constant interruptions. Is he gone? Another question I should've cleared was how long he would be visible, like this, as he put it.

Devin detected that I was edgy.

"Are you okay?" Devin asked.

"Not really."

I immediately fell prey due to the delicate tone of his question, but the reservations continued haunting.

"Are we okay?" Devin's face expressed that of a helpless, wounded animal.

"I need time, I guess. It's what Christian said, made me start thinking too much."

As Devin leaned in, poof, Christian was present.

"Miranda, I was wrong about him. I like him," Christian said.

I need not say that my mood changed in an instant for many reasons. Very important to me, Christian approved.

Tenderly, Devin rested his hands on my shoulders as he and Christian's voices blended together.

"What happened with my parents made me think that way," Christian said.

"Don't you think the situation with his parents made him think that way?" Devin asked.

The pleasure I felt was revealed in my smile.

****

Leaning on Nathan's shoulder, Pam drenched his shirt with tears. Out of her sight and shocked, Greer, stuck out his tongue out and shot Nathan the approving thumbs up.

His presence having been missing for four days, bringing the corridor to a detectable level of fear and anxiety, Trent quickly paced towards Pam, Nathan, and Greer. "Well, what a touching moment!" Trent shouted. Violently, he yanked Pam from Nathan's caring shoulder.

Nathan reacted, "Whoa pork chop."

"I was right about you all along, you whore." Trent jerked Pam around like a rag doll, and her crutches crashed to the floor.

Greer and Nathan glimpsed at each other and quickly hurled forward to protect Pam from the monster.

"Let go of her Big Bird!" Greer demanded.

Letting go of Pam, Trent snatched Greer by the shirt. At the same time, Nathan jumped up, latching himself onto the jock's bulky back, clasping he arms around his thick neck. "Let him go you big ham," Nathan tugged.

Saturated with the memory of a punch in the face, rolling across black asphalt, as well as the sound of metal crunching followed by rapid successions of emergency lights, Pam began screaming at the top range of her vocal ability. "Stop it!" The shout echoed in the slender corridor.

****

Hearing a high-pitched scream coming from down the hall that led to the auditorium, Devin and I rushed to find out what was happening. First, I thought something was on fire. Reaching the corridor, my heart began racing. Pam stood screaming, Nathan was clinging to Trent's back, and Greer was trying to rip his shirt off in order to escape a hand that was used to gripping sweaty footballs.

About the same time, on the other side of boy twister, Nana quickly shuffled forward dropping a bouquet of flowers. In one swift motion, Nana raised an umbrella, swung, and pegged Trent right in the middle of his nose. His face already wounded, I heard him grunt as he knelt to floor while Nathan rode his back on the way down. His hand released Greer's shirt causing Greer to stumble a few steps forward.

Reaching for Pam's arm, I grabbed hold, pulling her several steps backwards to a safe distance. Christian appeared at my side. Then, a feeling that I can never fully express hit me like lightening and caused me to gasp, as Christian's arm quickly brushed against mine. Catching my breath, I continued pulling Pam further away from the drama.

"No wait." Still sobbing, Pam tore from me.

Pam moved nearer to where, in pain, her former partner was squatting on the floor doctoring his broken nose. Since the moment Pam heard his monstrous voice fill the corridor, she'd returned to that Saturday night—speeding down a highway to the location where a wreath now rested as a memorial for my dearest friend in the world. Pam was ready to speak the words she hadn't shared with anyone about that fateful night.

Sixteen

When the balled fist made contact with Pam's face, the pain shot through her body, and for a moment, she escaped herself in a sort of dizzying sensation. Coming out of it in a panic, fear for her life mounted, and with her hand already holding the door lever, Pam pulled and pushed the door against the resistance of the draft. Trent slammed his heavy foot on the brake pedal causing the car to heave downward in the front while the bright red taillights warned from behind. The tires below the cabin and in the rear squealed loudly, equaling the screaming tires from Christian's car as he tried to avoid hitting Pam's rapidly halting car.

From Pam's pleading cries to be let out of the car seconds before punching her, the monster decided to grant Pam's wish. "Fine! Get out bitch."

To the left rear of Pam's car, a car whirled in the air—a violent ballet of metal and flying glass performing in slow motion. At the same time, Pam's body spilled to the firm asphalt to the right of the car. Fragments of flying debris shot through the night sky and rained down on top of her. Coming to rest with her head facing left, Pam witnessed the last dance as Christian's bloodied, tattered, and torn body twisted through the sky. Her eyes followed as Christian and his car crashed to the boggy marsh in a final crescendo. Not even Pam detected a final grunt as Christian's vitals flat-lined and the last breath left his lungs.

Pam screamed a cry of desperation, and realizing that she had a broken leg, Pam summoned every ounce of her strength to drag her body across the two-lane road and onto the left side of the highway with her arms. Reaching Christian, his face unrecognizable, she was powerless to help him. If she could've helped, it wouldn't have mattered; he was dead.

By the time emergency services arrived, Pam was catatonic.

Trying to uncover the specifics about the crash, Trent explained in detail what happened. The details were *his*. The officer recounted very selective details for confirmation, but one important fact that Trent didn't correct was the officer's assumption that Pam was a passenger of the mangled muscle car.

"We all go to school together. I'm on the football team." Pretending to be in shock himself, one of the personalities fed the actor's clever lines to the unsuspecting police officers who jotted notes on a small pad. "I don't know if I can call home. I'm sure he would come and get me, but, see, well, my dad tends to have a few drinks in the afternoons while he is watching T.V., and I wouldn't want him out on the roads. You know, for everyone's safety."

"We understand, son. We're glad that you're one of the levelheaded teenagers. Tell you what: we have to go right by your house on the way back to the station. Here is your drivers' license. Give us a few minutes to finish up with the wrecker. Here take my coat. You can wait in the car and stay warm."

****

As Pam and Christian revealed the truth together with one voice, I felt like someone was punching me in the stomach.

"Trent pushed her," Christian stated.

"He pushed me out of that car," Pam cracked as she revealed the secret.

Each face in the corridor expressed bewilderment until the facts fully registered. I got it right away. What went down that night wasn't so cut and dry as Trent's story explained: Christian wasn't merely following too closely.

With no reservation, Pam drew back a crutch and hit Trent. Reacting, the monster reached out and snatched Pam's injured leg. Losing her balance, Pam's body tilted backwards, and I moved in to steady her. Trent released his hold once Nathan's foot impaled him square in the ribs. Nathan dealt another blow just for safe measure. Once again, I backed Pam away to safety.

"Don't come near her again! And get some help, you big hog!" Nathan's pubescent voice cracked.

Devin positioned himself next to Nathan; I surmise he did so to protect Nathan in case Trent lurched towards Nathan. Nathan's scrawny arms were no match. This was the first time I had ever thought Nathan had a clue about what was going on. Most times, he seemed like he was on another planet. Perhaps he was brighter than I'd given him credit for.

Getting closer, Nana reached down, and using her fingers, she clinched a tender section of Trent's ear, guiding him to a standing-squatting position. With a large smile, Nana motioned to Greer and Nathan. "Can you gentlemen follow me to take this out of here?"

Nathan and Greer latched to Nana's side.

"Not so tough now are you tough guy," Nathan teased.

Pain shot through Trent's nose from the motion of the waddle. "Ouch, ow, Ouch."

Greer flicked Trent's free ear. "Big baby."

"Boy, don't tease the animals in the zoo," Nana said.

As Nana, my brother, and his airhead friend led Trent down one end of the hallway, Devin, Pam, and I headed backstage. Frenzied, Mr.

Stancil scooted through the dressing area whispering, “It’s time.”

We sat Pam down in a chair and she collected herself. Behind her, Christian’s hands appeared to hover, almost resting on Pam’s shoulder. Along with that and something I’m getting used to, they spoke in unison.

“She’s not going back to him.”

“No more. No more.” Looking down, Pam paused.

“No more.” Christian vanished.

Pam veered up. “No more.”

I soothed her hands “No more,” I said to Pam.

I felt Devin’s hand rest on the small of my back.

****

“See Dude, I knew that ham hock was a tool.”

“For once Nathan, you were right,” Greer said.

Bumping knuckles, along with Nana, they returned to their seats in the auditorium.

“Were have you guys been?” Miranda’s mother questioned.

Causing Greer and Nathan to laugh, Nana answered, “Oh, we had to take out the trash.”

“Mother, really.”

“Stop calling me Mother!”

“Now, all I got to do is score a phone number,” Nathan said.

“Nathan, you don’t drive. How are you going to take her out? I don’t think a girl like that would be too keen on the idea of having your parents cart you around town,” Nana said.

“I’ll teach her how to ride a skateboard,” Nathan replied.

“Oh, come on. Get real,” Greer said.

“Oh yeah, I forgot. You’re right, Greer. I’ll have to wait until her leg heals. Do you have an extra helmet?”

“Let her use yours. Your watermelon is hard as rock.”

****

The lights dimmed, and Devin was positioned to go onstage. "Good luck," he whispered.

"I can't feel my toes."

Pam snickered. "It's a good thing you don't sing with your toes."

"Are you sure you won't change your mind?" I asked her.

I knew she wouldn't, especially after what just happened. She simply nodded no.

Devin slid behind the curtain. This was it. The time had come, and a voice calmed my nerves.

"Through math, through art—even through death we won't part."

On my cue, I joined Devin onstage.

In that moment, I noticed that the stage felt so much larger, whereas the audience, dotted with people, seemed much smaller. Positioning myself, Devin began to play the familiar tune I heard on the first day of rehearsal. On the note where I was supposed to start singing, I froze.

This isn't fair, I thought. Looking out into the stunned faces in the crowd, one shined above the rest. Dead center, Christian's face beamed, and with his warming smile, he looked on. Pantomiming his feelings, Christian spelled out I love you. A lump captured my vocals, tears built, and as quickly as I blinked, Christian was gone. I raised my index finger to the crowd suggesting one minute.

I knew I would never see Christian again. I had, for lack of better way to describe it, a feeling. But along with that feeling, I knew he floated there within the layers of what eyes can't see. Even in death, we won't part.

As I left the stage, the pale murmur waved across the audience, and I couldn't help but suspect that a real emergency might interrupt the show, as Mr. Stancil was most likely in full cardiac arrest. Behind the curtain, I refused to take no for an answer while I forced Pam to join me onstage.

I'm confident I made the right decision because after the duo was over, the crowd irrupted with applause and cheers. In the orchestra area, I noticed Mr. Stancil jumping up and down a number of times as he spastically clasped his hands together. He was a part of what just happened: the magic of the music. Devin had climbed on top of the piano where he joined the celebration.

There were many more segments of the show, but we could have ended it right then, and I don't think anyone would have noticed. The universe was working magic in the theatre, and I like to believe that Christian had a small hand in the divine order of the night.

****

As the audience was breaking up, Nathan's eyes were fixed, and he remained oddly still.

Greer tapped Nathan on the leg. "That was boring as hell. Are you awake? What are you doing?"

"I can't move. I'm paralyzed," Nathan said.

"What?" Greer asked.

"I'm paralyzed with love."

Greer winced. "You, my friend, are paralyzed with stupid."

****

Backstage, Pam, Devin, and I embraced.

Devin was thrilled. "That was amazing."

"I still can't feel my toes."

"You were feeling something out there. I even felt it," Pam added.

It's obvious that Pam was happy that I had dragged her onstage.

Mr. Stancil scurried over to us, along with another gentleman who was wearing a tailored three-piece suit.

"Girls, I just don't know what to say. I couldn't have planned that any better myself. If that was secretly planned, then well done! I never pictured the story that way, but it worked. Though, if I do a rewrite, I will move that to the end of the story; that's where it should be. It even came across as symbolic. A girl survives a life filled with excess. A rebirth. Bravo. Oh, this is Mr. Steven Riley, with William Morris Endeavor."

SEVENTEEN

"Devin, I'm sorry."

"No, don't apologize. I completely understand. Should I assure you some more that I am not that kind of guy?"

"Hum. I have a secret source for information and a good feeling that I can trust you."

"Secret sources huh? Good. I like you. I really like you."

"I really like you too."

The sinful chocolate cake was calling our name after we parted from the school following the show, so we ended up on the stomping ground of our first date.

"That's pretty wild about Pam don't you think?" Devin asked.

"Could you imagine? I don't think that is a night that she will forget for the rest of her life. I mean how could she?"

"Right. She definitely needs to seek therapy."

"Like we said, therapy should be mandatory for everyone."

"Despite that nightmare in the breezeway..." Devin smiled. "Tonight turned out pretty well. How did you feel about Mr. Riley?"

"He was nice. Do you think that it's for real?"

"Miranda, I'm going to quote Ms. Nana. You're overly humble. You have a gift. It's time to share it. I think it was for real. Keep putting yourself out there."

"What chapter are you in right now?"

Devin chuckled. “Flattery. It’s an important chapter in the book. Didn’t Christian cover it?”

“I wish you could’ve gotten to know him. He was so much fun. You have no idea the crazy stuff he would say and do.”

“Well, if you don’t ever break up with me again, we have a long time for you to tell me all about him.”

“Do you know anything about those four-hundred and whatever number engines?”

“I don’t know anything about cars except how to drive them, put gas in them, and check the oil.”

“Well, Christian, like you, was very pretty, but he loved his car. Okay then. I’ll start by telling you about the pact he and I made when we were little. Not too long after we became best friends.”

Devin smiled as he reached for my hand and held it. “This should be interesting,” he said.

“Oh, it is. You might not even believe it by the time I get to the end, but it’s a very long story. Once I get to the end, you might be too old to care and even deny that it could be true.”

“Okay, I accept that proposition. Shoot, tell me the long story. I’ve got a lifetime to give.”

“Did we jump to chapter seventeen just now?”

“How about we start with chapter one of your story and forget all about that other book?”

“Agreed.”

****

Nathan fluffed the covering and slid his body into the sleeping bag. Next to the bed, Greer peeled his pants off.

“Dude, I didn’t need to see that,” Nathan said.

“Choke on a cheek chump.” Greer patted one side of his rear end and reached for the lamp switch. Greer sank down on the bed, stretching his legs out as he tugged the cover around his body. “Oh crap! What the hell is that?”

Getting out of bed, Greer peeled back the blankets, exposing the foot of the bed. The Jell-O shimmered while doing the wiggle and jiggle it is famous for.

“Dude, she got you!” Nathan howled, “Can I put the picture back on Facebook now?”

****

Deep in the throes of a book that had nothing to do with Devin or Christian, the shouts startled me from the pages.

Thickness of the walls muffled Greer’s cracking voice. “Miranda, I’m going to get you for this.”

I got him. Clever plan that Jell-O was.

I started laughing, and then I began to cry. Then I laughed, and then I cried some more. Those tears are tears of sadness and joy. What else could life throw my way after all that had happened?

****

Many weeks later, Devin, and I, with Pam in tow, visited Christian’s plot at the cemetery. I brought the wreath from the side of the road to place it in the appropriate spot. Devin and Pam agreed with me that it was morbid thing to do in the first place, and his resting spot was more appropriate than the side of the road.

Pam brought along a huge arrangement that her mother questioned endlessly about her need to buy. She did the best she could explaining, but Pam knew her unsympathetic mother would never understand even if she knew the truth about what happened that fatal night. Pam might tell her the facts about the accident, but in the future—after her recovery from her co-dependent behavior.

I held flowers as well and a handful of fun things to rest at the foot of the headstone. One item was a large can of Christian’s extra firm mousse that I swiped from his bathroom. So, that was the secret behind his orderly tresses! Next, I placed a laminated picture that was taken of Christian and me standing beside his car the day after he got it. Third, I positioned a playbill from our school musical. Finalizing the delivery, while I placed a laminated article from a local newspaper, Devin secured Christian's half of our friendship pendant with some permanent weatherproof adhesive just above the carved lettering of his name.

****

Holding the tiny piece of paper, Nathan's hand was sweating, and since he didn't believe it, his head was spinning.

Greer pried at Nathan's hand. "Let me see."

Nathan's fingers loosened one after the other, and Greer unfolded the sheet. "Holy shit!"

Nathan preened. "I had no doubts, you know?"

"Holy shit!" Greer said again.

"It was easy," Nathan said.

"What did you say?" Greer asked. "Holy shit!"

"I walked over to her, said hi, and asked her if she wanted to hang out with us."

"What did she say?"

"Nothing. She tore paper from a notebook, wrote on it, and handed it to me," Nathan replied.

"Holy shit! You did it dude," Greer said, amazed.

"Did you see it? Here, let me see it," Nathan said.

Greer held out his hand.

"See, P-A-M. And check it… check it out. Do you see that little heart she used as a period?"

"Holy shit."

"She is going to meet us there this afternoon."

"Holy shit."

"Dude, enough shitting already."

Outside the mall, Nathan and Greer spent hours teaching Pam how to use a skateboard. Pam was having so much fun, she lost track of time and failed to realize her mother was due to pick her up any minute.

As Pam's mother wheeled through the maze of parked cars in the mall lot, she caught site of her daughter across the way.

Pam's mother rolled down the window, peering across the sea of cars. "I'll kill her!"

A recognizable engine hummed as a car pulled alongside her car, blocking her view. The window of the muscle car rolled down.

"Evening. You don't see what you think you do."

A quick, bright light flashed in Pam's mother's eyes. When the muscle car pulled away, Pam was nowhere within view.

"It sure did look like her though." Pam's mother rolled up the window and carried on through the lot.

****

Since the flight was running behind schedule, we arrived at the offices of William Morris Endeavor exactly at our scheduled time. Mr. Ripley escorted us down a long breezeway to his office.

"Miranda you can sit here." Mr. Ripley pulled the chair out.

"Thank you," I said.

My mom, my dad, and Nana sat down in the remaining chairs, and Mr. Ripley situated himself at the head.

"This shouldn't take long and then you guys can enjoy the city. If you've never been here before, I have several recommendations for where we can grab some lunch courtesy of WME. Miranda, thank you for allowing us to represent you."

Back home, the whole town already knew the story since it was plastered all over the front pages of every local newspaper. I had laminated one of the articles and left it for Christian, though I suspected from wherever his viewpoint, he already knew about the headlines that read, 'Two local high school students discovered by a highly regarded talent scout from New York City.'

Mr. Ripley's assistant placed a stack of document in front of me.

My hand, slightly shaking, I lowered the pen toward the contract. Looking downward, the only thing in my view was an x, a long black line, and my full name, Miranda Leigh Owens. Resting quietly on the table, some clasped together, other tapping anxiously, were the hands of my mom, my dad, Nana, and Greer. When the ink pen nearly touched the blaring white sheet, I paused. A hand to my right eased in my direction and rested on my free arm. Nana made the supportive gesture to calm my nerves. I love that about her. Despite the motion of comfort, my thoughts wandered back to the point that got me here in the first place. Then I faintly heard, "Always here" in a familiar voice.

#

Cover Biographies

Cate Petteway—Cate's love and passion for acting has been part of her life since she was very little. From school plays to musicals and theatre to now film and TV, her talent to play a variety of characters, her professionalism, and her love for her fellow actors is what makes her stand out. Cate portrays Miranda in the short film "Always Here."

Gabbi Fairey—At a young age Gabbi discovered her passion for acting and has enjoyed theatre since the age of ten. She won 1st place a state competition for her role as Banshee in the musical, "Starmites." Gabbi enjoys challenging roles such as Charlotte in the film "Always," a period piece filmed in July of 2016. Gabbi portrays the character Pam in "Always Here."

Javy Barahona—With a background in TV/Film, Javy has played roles from the annoying younger brother, the witty class clown, a mythological Greek being, to an average high school skater boy, adding a little dose of comedy any chance he gets in various films, web series, and soap operas. In "Always Here," Javy serves as the character Nathan.

Jonathan Matthews—As the character Christian, Jonathan is making his onscreen debut in the short film "Always Here". Jonathan has performed in 9 different live shows spanning over a 4 year career. He is active with his high school theater troupe and has performed with the Holly Theatre Company. Some of his previous roles include an introverted high school nerd, an overactive attention seeking cat, and a Scrooge-like angry businessman. Jonathan also enjoys singing, photography, and writing in his spare time.

TONY VELLER—An Ohio native, Tony started his acting journey in 2016. After co-teaching acting classes with his mentor, he decided to pursue acting full time. His love for his craft has landed him a few roles in short films and a webseries. For him acting has become a way of life and he is excited to take on more opportunities. In "Always Here," Tony takes on the role of Trent.

TY REDNER—If Brad Pitt and Will Ferrell had a child it would be Ty Redner. Ty not only aspires to play a complex leading character like Pitt as Billy Beane in Moneyball, but also enjoys summoning his inner Will Ferrell which usually leaves an audience needing Depends. Ty loves being outside and riding his longboard. He also loves working with kids and volunteers at his church bringing laughter and Christ to the younger generation. Ty started his acting career at the tender age of five and has done numerous commercials and short films and plans to make a career out of bringing laughter and entertainment to the world by either being in front of or behind the camera. Ty humorously cover the role of Greer in "Always Here."

Made in the USA
Columbia, SC
08 March 2018